T0113707

Dreaming in Colour

Dreaming in Colour

Uvile Ximba

Published in 2021 by Modjaji Books
Cape Town, South Africa
www.modjajibooks.co.za

Edited by Mary Armour
Cover artwork by Edinah Tanya Chag
Book layout and cover design by Andy Thesen
Set in Legacy

ISBN print: 978-1-928433-17-0
ISBN ebook: 978-1-928433-18-7

This work is based on research supported by
the National Institutute for the Humanities
and Social Sciences.

To the people who helped me
write this book.

1
First dream

"Tea?"

She was wearing a navy, knee-length skirt that danced around her hips and the yellow, v-neck t-shirt complemented her dark complexion. Thuli, she had said I should call her. That was the first thing that had surprised me. How easy and light-hearted she was. As if the yellow of her top infused itself into her mood. There were smiles all round.

All broad smile and gleaming white teeth, she grinned down at me. "Tea, Langa?"

It was one of those thickly hot days when it felt as if the sun was sitting on the living room sofa. The windows were open and a slight breeze brushed the curtains back and forth. I had been airing my armpits slightly every few moments to let a breeze dry up the clamminess there. Steam rose from the spout of the teapot.

"Yes, I'd love some tea, ma –" I remembered her request, "Thuli."

A giggle tickled her throat and she smiled at me again. Her living room was a neat, generic space: white sofas, a red carpet and tinges of both colours matched in the cushions and frames on the wall. The glass table was pristine and uncluttered. I noted the dedication to cleanliness.

Thuli's daughter, uKhwezi, was hidden in the armchair next to mine, curled up and quietly watching us both.

"So what's this you want to talk to me about?" Thuli asked, settling onto the sofa opposite Khwezi and myself. Her question reminded me of the many visits to therapy I'd made. An open-ended yet leading question.

I glanced at uKhwezi. She looked back at me as she shifted forward to the edge of her seat. I could see the question floating in her head, the fantasy of the moment, her tense jaws working against one another. We had rehearsed this conversation together for the past week, anticipating every possible reaction her mother Thuli might have to the question's answer. Driving to the house earlier, a street away, Khwezi had pulled onto the pavement. The car's engine had trembled beneath us, mimicking her nervousness.

"Ask me again."

Now I glanced at Khwezi. Her eyes looked past mine, into those of her mother. Everything was yellow; the sun washing through the windows, bouncing off surfaces onto our retinas.

Thuli giggled once more, that light infectious laugh: "Ask you again?"

Khwezi nodded.

Thuli repeated: "What would you like to talk to me about?"

I melted back deep into my chair, nervous, trying to give them space yet watching both of them closely.

⁘ ⁘ ⁘

Awakening.

Khwezi's eyes blinked and stuttered open. She shut them again against the light filtering through the curtains.

"Khwezi! Vuka!" I descended onto her, ripping the blankets off the bed, and levelling my face close to hers.

"Whaaat?" she moaned, her eyelids sliding apart. I could see the grey dot-dots in her eyes, like swimming fish in a bowl of milk. With one a bigger brown whale.

"I had a dream," I announced.

"That's what most people do when they sleep, no?"

"Hmmmmm, mmmmm." My dreadlocks flew from side to side as I shook my head, "Not like this dream, Khwezi."

I let her climb out of bed and head for the toilet, knowing I could make her turn back any moment. Her long, lean legs sliced across the room as her sleep-dulled feet greeted the ground for the day. She stretched the sleep out of her back, light casting shadows along the grooves in her body. When she reached the bathroom door, I opened up. "It was about your mother."

As expected, she stopped and turned towards me: "Uh-huh?"

I nodded towards the empty space on the bed, beckoning her back to me. She defied me and slid into the bathroom. A steady stream of water tinkled loudly, followed by the whisper of toilet paper.

"Do you want coffee first?" she called out.

I made really bad coffee, tea, anything hot. Even my grandmother, uGogo Zonto – Lover of Hot Drinks – often refused to drink anything that was the spawn of me and a kettle.

"Sure. After I tell you."

Following another stream of running water from the tap, she paraded back to the bed. I could tell by the way she pulled up the blankets that she was irritated I'd woken her up.

"Okay?" she mumbled.

Intently, she sat there, listening to me unfold the soft, happy yellow dream of her coming out to her mother. Her eyes swam with the motes drifting through gaps in her mother's red curtains. They spilled over when I relayed her dream mother's blessing. Silently, she rose, stood above me and laughed.

uGogo Zonto always used to speak about her dreams. Indirectly to me, but more deliberately to others. Fragments would present themselves while I offered tea and spoonfuls of sugar, and cleared away plates of uneaten food. When her church and stokvel friends came over, I knew to hang around the door because they shared all the juice in whispers. If I didn't catch the gist of those murmurs and whispers, I would end up fishing out only the skimpy leftovers of the story amidst exclamations of awe and dismay.

"Jehova!"

"Hawu!"

"Unamanga Zonto".

I knew all the different symbols and metaphors that mattered in dreams. Snakes were trouble and danger, not a good thing to dream about. Fish were carriers of fertility and often associated with pregnancy. Death, ironically, was a good omen. Listening to my grandmother say to her friends, "Ngiphuphe uJoyce eshada", was often the highlight of my day. Although this didn't bode well for uJoyce, as her marriage spelled out only doom.

For me, sleep has always presaged a fortune-teller. Dreams have always meant something to do with the future, possibility or danger. Dreams are to be taken seriously.

Yet uKhwezi stood in front of me, rocking back and forth, her body a vibrating maraca of laughter.

"Yini ngawe?" I asked, annoyed.

She paused briefly, looking at me before cackling again, "Yellow? My mother hates yellow!"

"Ngi-serious, Khwezi, mani. It just makes sense. I think it's time that –"

"Because you dreamed about it. Really?"

She had stopped laughing and was now glaring at me. An argument was brewing in her lip, making it quiver. I could see her tongue straining against the gaps in her teeth, ready to defend her position. Opting not to answer, I nodded, returning a softer gaze. She shook her dread-locked head.

"I'm going to make coffee."

I watched her saunter to the kitchen before she added defensively, "Want some?"

"Come on Khwezi. I'm trying to explain ..." She shook her head again. "Okay, ke. Tea," I conceded.

The curtains in our bachelor flat were all slightly parted, welcoming in muted sounds of Makhanda street life outside. Flopping over onto my stomach, I spied on the world through one of the openings. Our space was on New Street, directly opposite Butch's Liquor Store a few addresses away from student nightlife spots. A pair of birds, a couple, flew onto the window sill, pecking playfully at each other and twittering. We all three looked down at the empty street. It was Sunday. Shops were closed and the town was heavy with a vodka-beer-boxed-wine babalaasz.

The smell of coffee and brewed berries crept up from behind me. Two mugs hovered above me as I turned. I took the one Khwezi thrust towards me and moved over so she could join me on the bed. The sound of me sipping berry tea was punctuated by the clink of her teaspoon as she slid it along her mug's rim, skating on the edge.

"Not right now," she said.

I nodded.

Coming Out Alone

Some people say the ocean isn't blue, that the water simply mimics the sky. That makes sense to me. Ocean water in Coca-Cola bottles is not blue.

But then what about when the ocean is green, turquoise, or teal? And the sky is blue? Or red?

I think the ocean is both the sun and the sky. The light and all the darkness. All the shades of yellow and blue.

2
Reading colours

Matric dance is a big deal. Everyone insisted I see that, scolded me when I expressed uncertainty about attending, predicted I would live to regret being absent from one of our biggest rites of passage.

For months, everyone at school and at home obsessed over dresses and hair, over make-up and glamorous hired transport. In something reminiscent of a wedding, the question on most lips was who was proposing to whom: "Who is X bringing as their date?" For months, girls sipped concoctions of cayenne pepper and maple syrup, vowing that it was Beyoncé's solution to their weight-loss problems. Those were the months I spent getting to know Khwezi.

The dance was set for the following Saturday night: the weather forecast predicted a warm evening. On Monday morning, an announcement resounded through the school corridors: the principal wished to speak to the matriculants during breaktime. At 1.30 p.m., we were herded into the hall, speculating in whispers about the reason for the summons. People settled into blue-uniformed groups, nibbling and slurping their diet-conscious Herbalife smoothies as we waited. Conversations paused and reignited.

"She's late," I said to Khwezi who sat beside me, her mouth a gaping gateway for her trucker burger. No dieting there.

"Yeah," Khwezi mumbled through her mouthful. "She is always late."

"Yet," I imitated the principal's snooty tone, "we at x-GHS strive to teach our girls to be punctual."

On cue, and almost defiantly, the principal strode into the room in heels. A stout woman in her fifties, her quivering upturned nose guided her forward. It twitched as she stood before us, shoulders back, head upright, chin upturned and out in a posture to rival any drama student. She prided herself on always maintaining an admirable posture. I wouldn't have been surprised if the talk was to inform us that we were all to attend compulsory posture-proficiency workshops before the dance. After all, the ideal x-GHS girl must present herself with postural grace and etiquette as a representative of the school.

"Afternoon, girls. I am sorry for taking up your free time. We," – she gestured towards the matriculant teachers who had slithered into a line behind her – "we feel that today is a convenient time to speak to you about the forthcoming event and the conduct we expect from all of you."

A whisper-wave undulated through the hall, broken by pockets of laughter and snickering.

"In particular, we need to discuss the issue of suitable conduct with the partners you bring.

She paused, held up a warning hand. Frowned.

Girls ... You are adults now and there are certain ... realities that you must be aware of. That is why we will be monitoring each and every one of you. *Prok-si-mi-tee*. No one is to stand, nor sit, closer than thirty centimetres to the boys, except when the official photographs are taken." Another wave of hilarity erupted from the students.

"X-girls are respectable ladies. Not promiscuous, uhm, uhm ..."

She stuttered over the thought. I could see her mouth working tensely around the unladylike epithets dancing on her lips.

"Bitches?" came a suggestion from somewhere close to me.

Her eyes squinted in my direction, "Excuse me?"

"Me?" My fingers pressed into my chest. uMama always said I spoke ngathi ngehla entabeni.

"I believe that's what you were going to say, ma'am?" Khwezi's cool penetrating voice strutted across the room.

I exhaled, not realising my lungs had been burning up with the breath I was holding in.

"That x-girls are not promiscuous bitches, ma'am?"

All the chewing halted. No slurps. All eyes focused on the principal. And on Khwezi, their head girl.

"I – no. Uhm, that is inappropriate and incorrect."

Her usual conviction was drowning beneath the truth of Khwezi's telepathy. That confident voice projecting right through the hall. Glancing around the room and back at the staff as though asking for assistance, the principal laboured on and floundered.

"That is unacceptable language."

Khwezi's calm gaze matched her voice: "I apologise for my assumption."

My own shock was duplicated in the expressions of those around me. The principal's rapid, flustered breathing was audible.

As an afterthought, Khwezi added, "Ma'am."

It was unlike the head girl to challenge authority. It was unheard of for anyone to challenge the principal's authority. Flushed, the principal ended the meeting and summoned Khwezi, before stomping out. As we milled around still gasping at Khwezi's deliberate insolence and defiance, we were handed pamphlets stipulating rules for the dance. The end of lunch was announced by the bell and everyone whispered their way to class.

That afternoon, Khwezi and I acknowledged one another quietly at the school gate, turning away from parents parked in convertibles and SUVs.

Cars whizzed past us and snatches of conversation rang out, then faded as we walked past quaint coffee shops and groups of schoolchildren on our way to the main road. Neither of us spoke as we eyed the red robot man, urging him to turn green. He did. We obeyed and crossed into the large park that wasn't too far from the school on our way to the taxi ranks.

"So?" My curiosity was choking me.

"She didn't say much. Only that she was disappointed. That as a student leader, such behaviour would not be tolerated from me."

"I can imagine," I replied. "She probably chastised you about how the word 'bitch' is an unacceptable term coming from the head girl of x."

Khwezi's laughter rippled across the park's lake, scaring a flock of birds into flight. They whirled into a hurricane above us, dispersing into the trees, squawking their discontent down at us. The path through the park unwound beneath our warming conversation and soon I could make out the traffic ahead. Sounds of honking and music from open windows blew at us between the trees' susurrations. Where the path ended, we trampled through fallen leaves, their muffled sighs punctuating our conversation with every step.

I spoke first.

"Everyone was so surprised. I may have heard a few people calling it impressive. Although I think that may be a push."

"Are you telling me you weren't even a little impressed?"

I rotated my hand in a casual swirl, the offhand gesture we used to describe something lukewarm or mediocre. Khwezi glared at me.

"Ngiyadlala hawu!"

She sneered triumphantly, "Unemusikanzwa."

"Huh?"

"Uyageza."

Taxis were now hooting close to us, the drivers looking hopefully in our direction. They crooked fingers out their windows at us as an invitation. We arrived at the small island of low-growing mushrooms we'd discovered on one of our walks. Khwezi reached for her phone as it buzzed through her pocket lining. Our parents' matric dance plans meant we should have been home earlier, but Khwezi tapped the silent profile on her screen and I knew neither of us wanted to leave yet. I settled noisily into the fallen leaf river and pulled out a nectarine from my bag to share. Khwezi joined me, sitting on the island near the mushrooms.

Blue is her favourite colour. That's what I remembered later on my way home. She said that was the one of two things she got to decide regarding her matric dance – the colour of her dress. Blue. That colour carried bad memories for me.

"What memories?" she asked.

I shook my head.

As we stood together on the concrete pavement, putting off the moment of separation, the sun set behind us. Everything was stained orange.

"What's the second thing you got to choose?"

Khwezi smiled quietly. A citrus smell lingered between us. In the dying rays, her eyes were a soft fire. A leaf wrinkled beneath her shoes as she stepped closer to me. We stood there, sharing again the orange in our breath. On our lips. Cars honked and drivers cursed, hurriedly opening their windows to swear on our eternal damnation. Jo'burg burned in the sunset, and us with it, at least according to the drivers in the traffic, who seemed to believe in Adam and Eve, not Steve, or however the saying goes.

The taxi I climbed into was clogged with KFC and BO and the faint smell of sweaty shoes. It had clearly been a long day. I greeted everyone with "Saniboni", still brazen from the excitement of our first kiss. Grinning to myself. The lady I settled next to, right in a front seat, beamed my feelings back to me. I wondered who had been kissing her that day. I drew my phone from my backpack and leaned my head against the cold window. The orange of the sunset was dulled by the greenish tint of the window, and everything looked slightly cold.

Already, a text from Khwezi waiting. Coolly, I typed back ...

> Whatssup?
>
> You're funny, she teased. Come here &
> I'll tell you! 👍

Almost immediately, my phone pinged again and I reached into my blazer pocket, pulling out my earphones to listen to the vn Khwezi had sent.

She had hopped onto a taxi she'd been on a few times. The driver, who called her "Schoolgirl", had noticed our hug goodbye and when she grinned hello, he'd asked if I was her girlfriend. There was a couple chatting and affectionately rubbing each other up in the back seat, a young guy in a brightly printed spottie in the front passenger seat and an older woman in a purple doek in the second row. Her purpled head had perked up a bit when he asked his leading question.

We hadn't spoken about it yet, so she'd shaken her head.

Laughing, he'd responded, "What are you waiting for? She is pretty, hey."

His friend in the front passenger seat had nodded enthusiastically and added, "Ya vele."

Khwezi texted me the summarised explanation she had given about her mother's opposition and how she had tried to tell her before about stuff without being heard. Almost in unison, her listeners sighed with disappointment. The chomi had mumbled and tweaked the front of his spottie to look at Khwezi more clearly, "Eish". The couple had fallen quiet.

"I think you should go for it. Umama wakho uzoba strong," piped the old woman. The conversation itself had made her lean forward to put her elbows onto the edge of the seat in front of her. Her eyes, firm and reassuring.

"It is not your mum's life."

The whole taxi nodded and groaned in agreement: "Yah."

"Sho."

"Hmmm."

"She must get with the times, your mother," added the girlfriend in the backseat.

"It is love. I saw it in the hug," the driver prophesied.

Another round of affirmations.

And the chomi chimed, "Yah, grand sharp. Sometimes the old people don't think we can love, uyacava? And bayakhohlwa ukuthi they were also here kissing and loving when they were young. You must get home, look at dimamzo in her eyes and tell her to find a nice uncle that will give her –"

"Hayi! Hayi! Hayi!" he was interrupted by the driver, "Don't teach Schoolgirl funny things. Lalela la, Schoolgirl," his gaze meeting Khwezi's eyes in the rear-view mirror, "just wait and enjoy the times with the other schoolgirl. And then one day, when you are ready, you can tell your mum. Neh?"

Khwezi said she'd nodded at him as she climbed out at her corner, thanking everyone for the advice before she walked off along the short path to her house.

⁂

Tuesday, the week of the dance. The suspense was building. School was unbearable.

> MD Rule #4: No learner will be allowed to bring another person of the same sex as their date. This includes any of their fellow schoolmates. Learners will be required to inform staff if they are bringing a female friend or family member and will have to submit a letter of approval from their parents before Thursday.

On Wednesday morning, I decided to go to therapy. The school therapist was a petite blonde woman with a close-cropped pixie cut, Halle Berry-style. Her office was cosy and colourful I thought, as I settled into a warm, brown leather armchair opposite her.

I briefly explained why I was there, that I'd been to therapy before. In a way I hadn't been honest with myself in all my life, I told her. I needed to be there facing things. I needed to feel fuller and more complete in myself. I said to her and to myself that I didn't want to rely on Khwezi to help me with that. This was my work on my own journey.

Whether trying to establish common ground, or simply talking, the therapist began to tell me about how she became an orphan. A tragic story, as loss tends to be. Her outburst irritated me. I hadn't gone to be her listening ear. I'd gone to unpack my own difficulties, not to be burdened by her grief. She failed me and I knew at once I would not go back for another session. If she could be selfish, so could I.

"Selfish" was exactly what I needed to be, coming here to talk about what lay unresolved in the past and to find closure. It wasn't possible to reach out to here and now. What could this woman give me that I could not give myself, that my mother could not give me? How embarrassed I felt when I arrived home that evening to have sought compassion from a stranger, to have been rejected and overlooked. How badly I wished I could yell at my mother when she asked me how my day had gone.

"Fine," I moped instead. Monosyllabic. Everything was fine.

✦ ✦ ✦

Thursday, the week of the dance.

07:00

> Hi Khwezi. Not coming to school today
> and tomorrow. Just so you know.
> See you @ The 'Event of the year'.
> At 8pm sharp 🕘

✦ ✦ ✦

Friday, the day before the dance.

uMama and I separated as soon as we entered YDE (Young Designers Emporium), searching for an emergency substitute matric dance dress. Gogo Zonto, who was making my outfit, had called Thursday night, warning us she might not be able to finish before Saturday.

uMama immediately gravitated towards the spicy red section. Black drew my attention and I skimmed through the range of black dresses. Pink pop played from the speakers, resoundingly loud in the empty store. Two cashiers smiled as I crossed in front of the till to meet my mom again at the fitting rooms. She sat outside in the aisle as I slid in and out of garments.

Squeezing into my third mermaid-style frock, the ring of my mother's phone echoed through the empty changing rooms. The ring tune was followed by a baiting, teasing "Hmmmmm". For a moment I contemplated pretending I had not heard her.

Instead, I enquired: "Who's that?"

She was taunting me, trying to get me to show interest in what she had to say.

"It's just your cousin."

A trickster hid beneath her smooth nonchalance.

I added neutrally, elongating the vowel for emphasis, "Aaaaaaaaaand ...?"

Ordering me to come out in the next dress, she shifted the conversation as expected. uMama's tactics were well known to me. This was a game we'd played a number of times before. The cubicle door shrieked as I pulled it open, stepping out in a black open-back number with a vez'ithanga slit that threatened to expose my vulva. I knew she would be distracted by the hotness of the dress.

I approached her and said, "Why are you talking to Viwe?"

Maintaining her evasive scheme, my mother pointed ahead and twirled her index finger. I spun around slowly on the spot, allowing her enough time to admire her chosen dress. Her eyes twinkled as I turned back to her and I knew this was her favourite. She had described the dresses I'd chosen as "churchy".

"Yini wakhetha ngathi ungumam' umfundisi."

Sometimes, I was convinced we were in one of those romcoms where people swap bodies. Except that our situation was more permanent.

"MMMMM. MMMMM. MMMM." The approving sound buzzed through the aisle, bouncing off fluorescent-lit walls back to us. I knew exactly what her next line would be: "I didn't go through labour for nothing, heh! Beka nje ukuthi umuhle kanjani!"

Our laughter echoed back at us. Catching my breath, remembering my mission, I assumed a 'serious' look to let her know the mood had changed. My eyes rattled questions at her. Slowly, the laughter dwindled from her eyes, replaced by a mixture of shame and mischievousness. It was the same look my younger sister used when she was caught being naughty but believed she could barter away her punishment through clever argument.

"Jonga," her manoeuvring began. "Your cousin Viwe offered to accompany you to the dance. He heard you were taking your friend and figured you didn't have anyone else to go with."

Huffing and half-caught between laughing out loud and throwing a white-toddler-in-Woolworths-tantrum, I took another breath and answered in measured tones.

"uViwe doesn't call or text me. He doesn't even know when my birthday occurs. How would he begin to know that I 'don't have a date', Ma?"

The buzzing of the thick lights suddenly echoed louder in the quiet room.

"Mama?"

Beyond the dressing room, another brief conversation ensued followed by the metallic clink of sliding door locks and the clicking past of high heels. A small lady clumped into the aisle, her face buried under a heaped pile of clothing. She mumbled hello before pushing into a room and twisting the cubicle lock into place. We stared at one another, uMama and me, listening to the riding of zips and the shuffling of fabric as the woman changed clothes.

"Ma?"

She peeled her gaze away from mine and down to her phone as it pinged again. Time passed between us. The finger tapping on her screen carried her further away from our conversation. A bed of needles pressed under and up into the soles of my feet, the sensation spreading, piercing, then numbness travelled up my limbs into my head. White, fluorescent light splintered behind my eyes, an ethereal membrane of light shards between us. Wrinkles creased across my mother's face as she focused on ignoring me, her just-visible moustache twitching with the effort.

In the glaring white light and white walls of that dressing room aisle, we had become separate. She had become to me like the woman in the cubicle, unfamiliar to both of us. A stranger.

Driving home, I prepared to emerge crying and bloodied, thrust into a strange world, one in which my mother rejected me. Remnants of the sunset filtered through the windows, threaded scarlet, trickles of light. I felt buoyant, yet oddly constricted, as if I was stranded, floating inside my heartbeat.

"uKhwezi and I aren't friends."

Streetlights shivered on, shaking light onto the tarmac. The streets were unusually empty and silent. Tranquil. I watched my mother poke at the round ON/OFF radio button. She did not look at me as one of those chatty PM radio shows came on too loudly. I switched it off.

"uKhwezi and I are taking each other to matric dance because we want to go together. Not because we are friends."

The radio blathered on again. We drove in silence. Unexpectedly, she whispered, "I know."

So quiet were her words that they dissolved into the noise of the radio. My eyes roved over her, lingering over her mouth, hoping to hear them uttered again, more steadily. I knew she could feel my gaze on her, yet her eyes remained on the road. It was a weird limbo; looking for the first time together as one, yet reeling mutely and as separate individuals. I wondered if this was what it felt like to be dead, whether you looked through reality and saw everything sharper and more clearly, witnessed all the disappointment and sorrow from behind a veil where nobody could see you.

Saturday evening was colder than expected. Betrayal and disappointment was on the lips and expressions of the students swarming into the hall; how dare the weather forecasts not live up to their promise? There were those who braved the chill, parading into the venue in flesh-baring attire. Others opted for shawls and coats, integrating the colours of these coverings into "the look". Despite this unwelcoming aspect, the cold wind blew full of expectation and celebratory anxiety.

With arms looped, everyone chattered with excitement going through the foyer. Clips of laughter and conversation were flung out in the wind towards us as Khwezi and I slid out of the car onto the drive. uGogo Zonto had managed to sew my black-and-white two-piece in time, a high slit riding up my thigh to reveal a red inner lining. Khwezi's strapless shift in turquoise silk shimmered in the light; aquatic, somatic, liquid in the air. We were late and the parking lot was empty as we crossed to the entrance.

I felt abnormally nervous and told her so. She smiled knowingly, wrapping her arms around my back and pulling me towards her. Her lips tasted like Colgate. I knew mine reeked of gin. A nod at one another and her hand in mine, we marched in. Beneath coloured lights, combined with the brilliant jumble of dresses and lively voices, the room was an auditory and visual rainbow that muted as soon as we stepped in. Arriving together meant breaking Rule #4.

Everybody watched as the principal stormed towards us, harsh disco-red light strobes slashing livid across her face. Tastefully, and of course tactfully, we were escorted out; security instructed not to allow us back inside.

We stood there out in the cold, staring at the slammed doors. The nasty weather was not compassionate and the security guards gave us pitying glances.

"Gin?" I offered, sneaking the bottle from my bag. Khwezi only looked at me, as if engraving me behind her eyes. Her Colgate smile. Downing large gulps, I handed it to her.

"How about some music?" She gagged a little as she swallowed. Translucent phone light illuminated her face; matching turquoise eyeshadow and nude lipstick. Her phone tucked between her breasts, she tugged me onto the now-empty drive.

"Come!" Khwezi began to dance. Very well, futhi.

"Yoooooh! Hayi!" I laughed, staring at her arms and legs moving skilfully all about. "Angikwazi ukujaiva."

She pulled me towards her, spreading my arms about. A dance puppeteer. It must have been the gin, I was suddenly so hot.

"I can teach you."

The security guards cheered as we danced, chuckling with us as we gyrated in our fancy dresses. We spent the night keeping company with them, Qiniso and Thuto. When we left, I thanked them. No one inside the hall had dared show us the kindness they did.

◆ ◆ ◆

That weekend, the principal barged heatedly into my dreams, descending upon a garden of flames, scarlet rosebuds that wilted and reignited, withered away only to burst into flame again. She was wearing the two-piece my grandmother had made for me and, from the flaming air around us, she drew a knife. She slashed at the dress as she drew closer to me, and a rumble of footsteps vibrated beneath us. All around me, classmates in cut-up, glamorous dresses sprinted away as they tried to escape a fire that wrapped itself in folds of their accessories, crept into the glossy patterned fabric of their gowns and seemed to burn them up alive from the inside. Boils of tormented flesh sprouted like flower buds and leaked blood. As I watched, the blackened and bleeding bodies grew again like phoenixes from their ashes, mimicking the roses about them. Oddly, the flames did not roar and only the girls' open mouths screamed torture. Their voices were all one, the anguished voice of Khwezi wailing: "We should not have broken rule number 4! We should not have broken rule number 4. We should not have ... We should not have ..."

Khwezi did not answer my calls all weekend.

3
After the dance

Early morning, Monday.

Spring was patiently colouring the trees back in. Curious prying eyes followed me through the school gates, hands covering mouths. It was the same on the bus. Stage whispers, too. No one was trying to hide that they knew something and that they wanted me to know that they knew. At the end of the long driveway, on the bench we always shared, sat Khwezi.

All alone.

"No secret admirers today?" I joked, finally approaching her past the barrier of stares.

Her back was turned to me, she sat bent motionless over the concrete table that matched the grey of the bench. If her shoulders and spine hadn't stiffened as I spoke, I would have thought her asleep. A gust of wind blew jacaranda blossoms off the tarmac, the last cold winds of winter.

It lifted them to a momentary stillness above us, before gently releasing them in a soothing, purple drizzle. A falling petal grazed the back of her neck and she finally turned to me, although staring away at the fallen mauveness.

"Kwenzakalani, Khwezi?"

We watched the last of the flowers tumble and melt onto the ground.

"She threatened to tell my parents, said she was certain my God-fearing mother could not possibly condone this ... condition."

Khwezi had made it clear how she thought her family would feel about her being with me, with any woman. She had also told me that the time for her to tell them, especially her mother, would only come much later, maybe after university when she was financially independent. I had said this was okay, that I could wait a while.

"So ... Manje ... What's gonna happen?"

Her eyes, red and swollen with tears, looked up from the purple carpet, took me in. She gazed at me the same way she had done Friday night, as if trying to sketch me into her memory. It was the same look, yet somehow different. A new silence closed between us as I sat next to her.

"I have to go to therapy. Or they will tell my parents."

"Therapy? For what exactly, Khwezi?"

"'To make me better'."

An afterthought: "Apparently."

Anger. The fury was stamping around in my stomach, an enraged beast. What Khwezi was saying was unbelievable, but even more shocking to me was how calm she was.

"Yikaka lena Khwezi! Absolute shit! They can't do this, dude! It's against so many things. Yi-discrimination lena mani!"

She just sat there looking at me.

"Kwenzeka ntoni ngawe, Khwezi mani!"

"Langa."

Irritation and frustration welled up in me: "Yintoni Khwezi?"

"We can't keep seeing each other anymore."

The school bell shrieked. A cluster of giggles, lines of students dwindling into their classes. Probably a vine. A cat video for amusement. I wanted to be one of them, oblivious.

Khwezi stood up quietly, tossing her school bag onto her back: "This is not right."

With the jacaranda blossoms falling, and those already fallen lying on the drive in pools of mauve, a solemn beauty settled onto the school.

Without a word, she left.

She left me.

◆ ◆ ◆

New rules were announced by the principal at that morning's assembly. They would not be published in the school's Code of Conduct. However, it was made clear that we were to adhere to them. A cluster of girls snickered.

She repeated the fifth rule, for which the preceding rules were like subtitles:

"Gutter behaviour is unacceptable. Girls, we are not a Pick n Pay shop floor. If you do not want to behave appropriately, there are shebeens and township schools where you can go loiter around."

A girl sitting behind me cackled, "Do you think Khwezi shops at Woolworths or Pick n Pay, huh?"

Her friend laughed. "Woooo. Shem. Pick n Pay kuphi? Maybe Cambridge Food or Shoprite."

Anyone would have thought I had wheels rotating beneath me, that's how quickly I spun around. A handful of her hair in my grip, all my frustration and anger, my tears, Khwezi, my childhood, my father leaving, my being left behind, abandoned. It all surged into my open palm and landed across her face.

gutter behaviour (n.) 1. Behaviour or conduct that is promiscuous, inappropriate or unladylike. This includes any kind of contact between students. **2.** Behaviour or conduct that does not align with x-GHS decorum. This includes sexuality, homosexuality, explicit enjoyment and emotion of any form, loudness ... **1.** Trashy (**adj.**)(COLLOQ.) **2.** Ratchet (**v.**)(COLLOQ.) **3.** Indirect allusion to all behaviour that does not align with white decorum. **E.g.** This school is not Pick n Pay. We will not condone gutter behaviour. Go enjoy your gutter behaviour in shebeens.

I cried in the school bathroom, waiting to go into the principal's office.

E.g. Giving a bitch a hot klap in the middle of a school assembly. Even if they deserve it.

✦ ✦ ✦

I do not cry as I climb into my mother's car, and she shouts, "SUSPENDED?" Instead I cross my heart and hope that all the ghosts of social activism will descend on that South African girls' school. All my ancestors, too, the ones who are not homophobic, will teach these white people what gutter behaviour is. They will know who I really am. I am livid with rage.

During the two weeks of my suspension from class, all I can think of, all I hear is Khwezi spitting out, "This is not right!" Accompanied by jacarandas weeping blue in my sleep.

✦ ✦ ✦

uMama and I are close. Well, at least we get along. She clothes and feeds me. Has raised me on her own. Carried me on her own. She shouts at me for getting kicked out of school.

"This is not how they must see us," she says.

uMama loves me, even when she feels I am difficult to love, even when she doesn't understand. This is something not all parents know how to do.

✦ ✦ ✦

Suspension over, I returned to school. Khwezi was waiting for me at the entrance gate. *Typical*, I groaned inwardly, *the entire school probably knew I was getting back today*. Over the fortnight, I'd thought I'd missed her. Sadness engulfed me as I neared her. Anger, too. Outrage. And something else I didn't want to feel.

"I'm sorry," she began.

Walking past her: "I know."

There are so many things I fear. One of them is being left behind. I am scared of all the people that can leave me.

Eventually, I said to Khwezi, "I'm sorry too. I know it's difficult and I don't expect you to come out. Not for me right now, at least. But sometimes that decision is not an excuse. Especially for how cold you chose to be towards me. That was your choice. Not theirs."

✦ ✦ ✦

There were so many things we couldn't do anymore, things that weren't made explicit or stipulated in the school newsletter or in the Code of Conduct in case the more liberal white parents read them and withdrew contributions.

We couldn't hug one another, or hold hands. Two girls were caught staring at one other "too long, too intimately" in class and sent to the principal's office.

No girls could shave their heads. This would make them look masculine and unattractive.

Our school dresses had to reach below the knee and be a loose fit. Our parents were informed about this ruling because they had to pay for new uniforms. What parents didn't know was that many black girls were singled out for criticism because we had "prominent body types". Short or small dresses, too-tight dresses, sent out the wrong impression. If we couldn't afford new ones, there was a charity room with secondhand uniforms available. That's what I was told.

Maybe that's why Khwezi succumbed (they said in accusatory tones), because of all my curves.

Maybe this was the way they could prevent any more attractions.

Khwezi drafted a list of complaints as a response and persuaded most of the girls to sign it. The emailed official response from staff was evasive but final.

"The matter does not correlate in any way to race. What is important is appropriate physical appearance."

We did not think that we could fight further. We knew about systematic racism but we did not know that it was also making us pat down our afros or that buying looser dresses counted, or being told to go back to township schools, or that our parents didn't attend meetings because they were busy hanging out in shebeens.

When we arrived at school late, we were told that having to catch unreliable buses and taxis was not a good enough excuse. "*Wake up earlier.* This is why we don't accept people who live far away. They don't participate fully in school activities, they don't help to build the x-girl community."

And although we also knew about sexual harassment, we didn't think that being called "sluts" counted, or being shamed for falling pregnant, or being "gay", or having too-thick thighs or voluptuous breasts.

Instead, we learned to focus on the privilege of being in a "good school". Subconsciously, we stopped wearing short or clingy skirts, even outside of school. We focused on Physics, Maths and Accounting so we could be "better than Stephanie". And each day we said nothing to our parents, because, we told ourselves, there are students worse off than us. There's no time to be too sensitive. It's better to continue quietly hating who you are: black, queer and female. In that order. In any order.

⁂

"Yellow."

"My mother hates yellow."

"Okay."

"Sorry."

—— silence ——

Again, "Sorry. What I should have said is 'Why is that so?'"

I smiled: "That's okay. And I don't know. I guess not many things remind me of light. That's why I like yellow."

A question crept into her, lighting up her eyes: "Why's that?"

"Why is what?"

"Why do few things remind you of light?"

I ignored her curiosity, "Yours is blue, right?"

She smiled, "You remembered."

Blue reminds me a bit of death, I thought.

Instead, I asked: "How come?"

Dusty-grey birds stalked around us, their cries meeting and mixing with car honks and engines. iGqom pounded from a Quantum further down the park, cooler boxes and camp chairs gathered around its back.

Ayayayayayaaaaa! Yebo! Yeyi! I could imagine the cracking of knees as a series of iivosho circled through the small crowd. Saturday was definitely blooming.

Khwezi and I were sitting together under a willow by the lake. A few couples chirped from small boats wafting smoothly across the water. I picked at the dark green paint peeling off the bench we were sitting on. Placing her phone next to me, she said, "You start."

Hiding laughter behind a smile, I asked, "Don't you think this is a little bit cheesy, heh?"

Khwezi, confidently and firmly, "Yes. I'm cheesy. But you know that."

On number four of a magazine quiz headed 34 Questions for New Relationships: What is your favourite colour and why?

"Black," I answered, "And ... yellow."

"My mother hates yellow."

Khwezi barely spoke about her family, and when she did, it was never about her mother. I'd seen her mum once, parked in her mauve Audi A3. Khwezi had been roaming somewhere inside the school, probably still in one of her extra murals or heading a Prefects' meeting in the RCL room.

Khwezi's mum had stepped onto the pavement, placing her glimmering, studded heels tentatively, thoughtfully, onto the concrete. I thought, as she glided past the faded blue-star school badge emblazoned on the gate, that she walked as if every step was calculated. Had I not just seen Khwezi, I would have thought she had changed into a crimson bodycon, pulled on a wig and run into the bathroom for a handy face-beat. They were almost identical.

“Sorry,” Khwezi repeated, “What I should have said is ‘Why is that so?’”

Yellow is a light colour, I told her. We spoke about the colour blue, her favourite. Swiftly, the questions moved from clipped personal fun facts to extended, probing discoveries.

“What colour do you not like? Why? If it is attached to a memory, share this memory with your partner.”

Birds cawed. Oars broke water, the glugs echoing. Khwezi sighed faintly. I echoed her sighs stubbornly, refusing to lead this time.

silence

“Okay fine. I’ll go first.”

❖ ❖ ❖

Leaving the park, Khwezi blurted, “I don’t think your mother likes me anymore.”

Slivers of light danced across her face, glinting in her eyes. I caught my reflection in them, yellow in the sunlight. I’d just got off the phone with uMama.

“Your mum definitely doesn’t like me,” I poked back teasingly.

No response. Something had shifted in Khwezi as we’d finished the quiz. She was being uncharacteristically quiet. This was how she became when she was carrying a thought. She would lay it down with her as she went to bed, pull it around in her head through the day. Now, she was rolling it about, considering how to best unburden herself.

Certainly, it wasn’t as though I hadn’t noticed a shift in uMama’s treatment of Khwezi. Before, when she still believed we were only friends, her excitement and love of people had bubbled over onto Khwezi. She, uMama, would speak to Khwezi enthusiastically, and once we were on our own, would gush how she really liked Khwezi, how pretty she thought her. Since the week of matric dance, she had become more restrained. Now, when I'd told her I was still with Khwezi, she had been cold and abrupt, hurriedly ending the call.

I shared my observations with uKhwezi. Relieved not to have imagined the change, her informative eyes asked, "So, do you think she hates me?"

"Angazi."

"But what do you think?"

"I doooooon't knooooow," I shrugged, gluing my pupils onto hers, "Now are you gonna kiss me goodbye, or do you want to keep discussing my mother?"

I knew what Khwezi really wanted to know was what would happen if my mother didn't really accept us being together, whether we would come apart. I also knew she wouldn't ask me this because she herself wouldn't be able to answer me if I asked her the same thing.

✦ ✦ ✦

My younger sister Xola's excited voice ushered me into the house,

"What colour?"

Her paintbrush wrapped in her hand, she teetered towards me, spreading her arms around my knees and pulling me into the house.

e-Dining room, a coral pink glow seeped through the curtains into the room, flushing the beige sofas and white walls, the wall clock. Sheets of paper littered the brown and beige carpet, a rectangle of paints and brushes sitting in the centre.

She pulled me to kneel beside her. We hovered, our eyes darting across the options. Xola plugged her thumb into her mouth, the wet sucking noise irritating my inner ear. She was on the second-last page of her colouring book, a picture of an unusually large squirrel in front of a wooded forest. A brown sky poked out beyond the already purple-coloured trees.

"What colour?" she mumbled, stabbing the squirrel, "What colour do you want the rat?"

A few of the paint circles were cracked, others missing. I smiled, "It's not a rat. It's a squirrel aaaannnd I'd like ... GREEN!"

Swish, her arm shot out and hovered over the colour tray, searching for the right circle. A pause, followed by the faster, anxious shlup shlup shlup of her thumb.

A frown crinkled her eyebrows as she stared at the paints. The green circle was missing.

"You know," I pulled a paintbrush from the pack, dabbing it into the yellow, "if you mix yellow ... (dab) and blue ... then you get ... GREEN!"

She gurgled with laughter. "Yeeeeeeeeesssssss!"

Leaving her to attack the squirrel, I clicked on the TV.

"Sieeeeeeeeees!!!!!" she screeched, torn between giggling and gawking.

I began to explain to her that there was nothing wrong with what she was seeing. She must not be rude to people. "Those two people really like –"

"Langa!" uMama was annoyed. I hadn't heard her coming in from her room. Xola and I watched her nestle into the sofa behind us.

"Ndicela i-remote, Langa." I handed it to her. I watched as uXola filled in her green squirrel. uMama switched to the news.

21:00

Harriet Khoza was hurling commands at her family on TV and uXola had packed up to go to bed, hopping out of the room after hugging us both. I had a plan to soften the mood. My method: a spatter of gossip, a display of interest in her recent activities, and a cup of tea.

Before I could offer her the latter, she rose from the couch.

"Hayi. Ndiyonqenqa mna ngoku."

I had to just get to it: "Yima mama." She stopped rummaging for her phone between the sofa cushions. "Ikhona into endifuna ukukubuza yona."

"You can ask me anything ngomso, Langa. I am very tired."

Perhaps, my voice translated as anxious; I detected unease in hers.

Muting the TV, carefully, quickly, I blurted: "Do you not like uKhwezi anymore?"

Her measured breathing hissed through the room: "Why?"

"I've noticed you don't speak to her like you used to. You're colder." I paused, hesitated, "She's picked it up too."

More breathing. This time with no response. A chunk of time snailed by. I watched as the seconds ticked off on the wall clock behind her.

Finally: "I can't be friends with the person you're with. There just needs to be distance, even if you were dating a boy. That's all."

Tick. Tick. Tick. It was my turn to be disquieted. I wanted to believe her. My mum had always supported me and I'd always relied on her to do so. Genuinely. Yet something made me feel her trying to persuade herself to be there for me. Parts of me knew that she didn't really believe in what she was saying. Especially when she said Tick. Tick. Tick.

"It's not because she's a girl. I like her."

More to myself than her, it was my turn to measure my response: "Then how come you have a problem with uXola watching two women kiss on –"

"She is seven years old, LA-NGA! How can I let her see that ... THAT ... Those things?"

"So unayo inkinga ke, Ma?"

She sat down again. Mouths moved silently on the screen, the creaking of the house and the tswiri-tswiri of oomantswiri-tswiri from outside. Even the sound of her running her palms down her thighs seemed to echo in the room.

"It's just not normal, Langa." No hesitation. No disillusion. Only clarity and conviction.

"There is nothing not normal about it." I wished I was as confident, as clear as she was. Instead, my words escaped me in small whispers, "How is it not normal?"

She rose to search for her phone and finding it, said: "It's only normal for you because you're doing it. There's nothing normal about it. And," (she turned, hovering, glaring down at me) "I don't want you talking to my daughter about it."

I increased the volume on the TV and muttered: "Goodnight."

She left.

✦ ✦ ✦

Why did I feel so ashamed, I chided myself. After that night I felt wrong. I felt not right. *This is not right*. It is not, I thought. It cannot be if my mother can look through me, face scrunched up the way she pulls it out of shape, as if walking through the sewage-drenched CBD streets. How can any of this be right? What am I doing?

I ask Khwezi, "What are we doing?"

I can tell she feels dirty too, not right. I understand why she said it now.

"I don't know," she offers weakly, "Only God knows."

✦ ✦ ✦

Dawn came early the morning I was born and the day was too warm for April. Cradling me in her arms, as welcoming as the day, my mother always reminds me how she whispered her first words to her first-born daughter: "Mafungwashe, igama lakho lizakuba nguLanga – for the sun that accompanied you into the world, for all the light you bring with you."

✦ ✦ ✦

Mama,

Maybe that's why uTata left us?

Maybe he had a dream that warned him he would have a daughter that disappointed him?

✦ ✦ ✦

Mama,

Am I still the light?

Coming Out With Khwezi

*"You shall not lie with a male as with a woman.
It is an abomination."* Leviticus 18:22

4
Sex education

School can be the beginning of broken societies.

"Life Orientation class is a waste of time": the groaning complaint of South African high-school youth since 1994. It is a half-hearted and resourceless effort to "orientate" teenagers – of course – to adapt to the world outside home and school. You might think that this would involve basic knowledge about financial management (how to open a bank account) or investment. Perhaps, even more fundamental lessons like preparing all learners to pass their learner driver's licence. Instead, for four years, textbooks vomit mixed-up, propaganda-coloured perspectives on conflict-resolution and STDs. On sex.

After spending a quarter of my life making posters about gonorrhea and different types of contraception, this is what I thought I knew about sex before Khwezi:

1. Sex requires penile penetration. Without it, everything else is just messing around.
2. I cannot get pregnant if there is no penetration.
3. How to help The Guy put on a condom: my Life Orientation teacher from one of these years decided to demonstrate on a wooden dildo using a brightly coloured, scarlet CHOICE. Khwezi's hand shot up: "How do we put on female condoms?" The said teacher tried to camouflage herself with the dildo in her hand, her boiling-hot cheeks redder than the phallus.

4. That people on TV never put on condoms.
5. That people in porn videos never put on condoms.
6. That guys don't like using condoms.
7. I cannot get pregnant if I don't have sex. Remember penetration by a penis: THAT alone is sex.

This is what I knew.

uMama was a social worker and worked mostly with teenagers. She spoke openly about sex. Especially when we watched TV together: she'd talk about condom topics 4 and 6, about pregnancy, about the danger of penises. Never once did she or my teachers mention pleasure. Never did I get from their "advice" the guidance I would need to actually navigate and define sex for myself.

There were boys before Khwezi. A couple of girls I'd thought curiosity drove me to kiss. But mostly boys, with penises. Games of Spin the Bottle uncorked my relationship with their penises. Of course, there were turns that saw me kissing girls, but it was when the circle set on humans with penises that the atmosphere grew tense. Giggles and whispers. These encounters resounded more intensely within the group.

At some point, the game became redundant and I decided to limit my lips to someone I cared about. Girls were never ruled out but I was never short of attention from the boys. I was tactical and self-protective, though. Being shipped off to live with some or other family member because of teenage pregnancy was a possibility; a guarantee from my mother; a promise I didn't want to test. I stuck to my guns, allowing no fingers to stroke me long enough that I forgot the mandate: no babies. Blue-balls: I lived with them. Pleasure was just not worth the pregnancy. And certainly, though the lust was urgent, I thought that if I was willing to risk pregnancy, I should do it knowing I felt more than just lust. How not to have babies was what mattered.

✦ ✦ ✦

Before I began living with Khwezi, in first year at university, I shared a flat with Zikhona. Her men friends always came over, claimed the kitchen-cum-living room. When Khwezi was not there, they looked at me like I was a luscious ice cream they wanted to demolish. Their eyes licked me naked. When she was around, they retreated, spoke to her about soccer and hip-hop, the way men who usually make lecherous propositions and howl together obscenely are suddenly respectful when a woman is linked with any man.

"So how's the pussy?" they asked, "We hear you sometimes. From out here. "

When she told me this, I was ashamed. Of sex. Of enjoying it. I was ashamed. I stopped having sex when they were around.

Nobody must know you are having sex.

⁂

We went to a chillas one night in our second year with a bunch of people we thought we might kind of like to be friends with. One of them called us "Golden Lesbians - or something".

I punched him in the face.

Khwezi opened each of the six Black Label beer bottles he'd brought along and spat heartily into them, one by one. Isikhwehlela, hmmm.

That's what we should have done to Zikhona and her friends. But it was okay. At least we were defending ourselves now.

⁂

"Do you guys think dreams have meaning?"

About five or six people were gathered at our apartment. Black Label bottles, vodka and Sprite mixes and a few wine glasses were scattered around the kitchen and the cushion ring we'd created. We'd been talking. Just talking. And things were coming into hazy but mindful focus after a few shared drags off a joint.

We were talking about men. Even the men were talking about men, about themselves and about each other. I remembered the dream I had had about one of them, the men, one of the ones in that room.

Mavuso had cackled in that dream, "I know I gave it to you better than Khwezi, huh. I know I did."

Now, he answered my question confidently, "Yeah, they do. Of course, they do. Of course, dreams matter."

✦✦✦

Do you think dreams have meaning?

✦✦✦

The same set-up on another night.

A hearty aroma of grilled meat filled the apartment and Khwezi's party playlist livened up the apartment. Thato had just walked in and introduced us to her latest girlfriend, Bassie. They moved to sit in the living room after the greetings and I watched them giggling and caressing one another. I waved across the kitchen counter at Khwezi, trying to get her attention from the pot she was focused on preparing. When she glanced up, I winked over at the living room to the handsy couple. Khwezi grinned and winked back.

"Thato!" Khwezi called from the kitchen, "What were you guys doing before you came here?"

Thato laughed heartily and responded, "You know, wena."

We did know because they'd brought with them the smell of pre-drinks and sex. Bassie giggled nervously and Thato added, "Don't act like you didn't get the night started before we came here."

I watched Bassie visibly relax when I teased, "Of course we did."

Khwezi wrapped up her pap pot and grabbed drinks, wine and beer from the fridge, and glasses, spanking my bum on the way to the living room. I sipped on my Black Label and emptied the last tray of meat into a bowl before joining them in the living room.

"Where are Mathembi and Mavuso?" I asked.

We had invited Mavuso to bring his girlfriend Mathembi to the movie/dinner party. Although we were not extremely close to him, we enjoyed his company from time to time. He was Thato's close friend, though, so she answered, "He said he would be a bit late so I guess we can eat without them."

We were all sitting around the TV, filled up on pap, meat, gravy and booze, partly watching the movie but mostly catching up on nothing, when there was a knock on the door.

Mathembi's raspy voice followed, "Koko!"

"Come in, it's open!" Khwezi joked, heading to the locked door to open up. Mavuso burst into the room, loudly greeting us.

"Khwezi! How are you, bra? We're so late. Have you guys eaten? We're super hungry." His voice barged into the living room before him. "What are we watching, guys?"

Mathembi was his contrasting shadow, calmly and quietly greeting Khwezi, slinking into the semi-circle in front of the TV, accepting the beer Khwezi brought her from the kitchen. Mavuso settled next to Thato and Mathembi next to me. She smelled like a fragrant aerosol spray and Sta-Soft.

"It's good to see you again," I said to her, sipping my drink and watching her boyfriend out of the corner of my eye. He whispered for a long time into Thato's ear before making a gesture with his hands. He grinned enthusiastically as he did, and Thato smirked. His eyes caught mine and he laughed boisterously, no longer gesturing. My beer slipped from my hand and spilled onto the floor, lapping at the edge of Mathembi's pants. Mathembi and I both jumped.

"Ooops, sorry! Let me get a cloth," I apologised, snatching up the bottle from the floor and rushing into the kitchen. I ran a cloth under the tap, looking out the window above the sink into the dark sky outside. Hands wrapped around my waist, and I tensed slightly before realising it was Khwezi.

"Are you okay?" she whispered, nibbling my ear softly.

I purred, melting softly, and relaxing, "Yeah. I'm fine."

"Fine?" She rotated me in her arms so I was facing her and her hands slept gently on my behind. "*Fine* is usually not good at all with you. What's up?"

I didn't know why the exchange between Mavuso and Thatho had unnerved me. "I am not sure ... It's just ... I will tell you when I am sure."

She nodded, kissing me first on my cheek, then slowly on the mouth, and finally on my forehead, "Okay, you will tell me later then? We will need some pillow talk after dessert later."

I giggled, the feeling in my chest ebbing slightly and giving way to a rush in my stomach and loins. She pulled me closer and I kissed her, allowing my tongue to trace her lower lip before biting it gently.

As Khwezi released a low moan, Thato's voice teased, "Look who's getting handsy now!"

We both laughed and pulled apart, glancing at Thato who was getting fresh drinks and ice.

"When did you get in here, creepy?" Khwezi asked, to which Thato just smiled and winked.

"Khwezi," I whispered, making sure to keep my voice low enough that Thato wouldn't hear me as she was busy smacking the ice tray against the counter. "Can you please give me a chance to talk to Thato? I want to ask her something alone."

"Tjo, sounds serious ... and secretive! Okay, sharp. You can come sit on my lap when you come back." Again, she spun me, this time so I was facing Thato, and the spank she gave me prompted me forward.

"What are you drinking now?" Frowning at the wine-beer-spirit mix she was making. "Bassie said she can drink anything and I dared her she couldn't. So now I am trying to mix the most disgusting thing ever."

"Hayi, let me make myself a normal drink, mna."

I grabbed a glass and added ice and two shots of gin. "So, I noticed Mavuso was saying something to you earlier ... and he did a thing with his hands. What was that about?"

Thato continued creating her concoction, browsing through the cupboards at potential ingredients. "Oh, he does that all the time. I don't mind him. Doesn't he do it to you and Khwezi?"

"Do what?"

She paused and glanced at me. "The scissor thing."

I realised what the gesture was when she said that. He had spread two fingers on each hand to make symbolic scissors, and collided them against one another.

Thato continued, "He does it all the time, asks us if we butt vaginas, if that's how we have sex. I thought he did it to you guys, too. I didn't think it was a big deal."

I shook my head, "No, he doesn't do it to us. And it's not alright actually. Why don't you confront him about it? Doesn't it make you uncomfortable?"

She just shrugged and turned back to her muck-making, ending the conversation. I added tonic and more gin to my drink, returning to the group. As promised, Khwezi urged me onto her lap and I rested against her. I couldn't quite remember the movie we were watching but there was a woman running through the forest, screaming for help and weeping. A horror? Documentary, maybe.

"Mavuso, I saw what you were doing earlier with your hands when you were greeting Thato. What's that about?"

"Oh, that. That's nothing. Just a joke between me and my mngani, Thato."

It was nagging at me and I wasn't ready to let it go, "What makes you think it is funny? Does Thato think it's funny?"

He kept a wide grin on his face but I noticed a twitch of annoyance or anger in his eyes.

"We can ask her." His voice was no longer jovial.

The others were confused, and I explained to them what I'd witnessed as Thato occupied her spot again. She opened her eyes wide when Mavuso forcefully probed her about whether or not she found his style of greeting humorous.

I finished explaining. Khwezi scoffed, and added, "Jokes are meant to be funny, and this obviously isn't. Thato might not want to say anything but Langa and I certainly aren't comfortable with that happening in our space."

Not one for confrontation, Thato shrugged and pulled a long gulp of her drink. Shrugging, she quipped, " It doesn't matter guys. Let's leave it." The look she gave Khwezi and I begged us to let it be.

Khwezi inhaled deeply, not willing to let it pass, but Thato interrupted her, "I don't want us to ruin the night, please."

Mavuso relaxed visibly, an amusement replacing the simmering anger. Unapologetic, he jumped onto Thato's dismissal and turned the volume up on the movie that had disappeared into the background. I could hear Khwezi's raspy breath, upset and dissatisfied. She crossed her feet, uFour, a habit I knew meant she was working hard to keep her mouth shut, as though trapping her words in the triangle formed by her limbs.

The room suddenly felt smaller, the silent tension was broken only by the crunch of popcorn and shlurps from our drinks, glasses set down after sips, the uneasy shuffle of bodies. I caught Bassie glancing around uncomfortably, uncertain if this was how disagreements often played out in the group.

Mavuso was tapping his feet against the floor, the light clap of his inner thighs getting louder as his foot landed rapidly against the ground, lulling only to start again. All the sounds come together to form a soundtrack to the film, driven by the prickly tap, tap of Mavuso's feet.

Tap, tap, tap, tap.

Mavuso's soundtrack stopped, followed by an unnerving chuckle, ugly and mocking. Bassie had settled into Thato's arms, nestling into a cuddle that Thato sealed with a kiss on Bassie's forehead. We all watched Mavuso shake his head "mxm" at Bassie and Thato wrapped up in each other.

"Is there a problem?" Khwezi poked, taking the opportunity to finish what was started.

Shockingly, Mavuso hopped up onto his feet, wagging a stubby finger at us, and shouting, "No way guys. We're not gonna do this right now."

Before Khwezi could respond, I rose and asked, "When exactly are we going to do this, father?"

He barked a shrill laugh, bent down and reached for the remote, switching off the TV and declaring, "We don't need to talk about this ... shit, right now."

His statement would not have meant a thing if he hadn't nodded his head in Thato's direction when he said "shit". This fanned Khwezi's flame and she stood up next to me, "So Thato and Bassie cuddling is shit?"

Mathembi had slid up to stand quietly behind Mavuso. Bassie sat upright next to Thato who had her head in her hands.

"No, no, no," Mavuso threatened, edging towards us, waving the remote in our direction. Khwezi reached for the remote and Mathembi swiftly knotted his hand around her wrist, wringing it hard.

In a barely audible whisper, Khwezi spat, "Let me go, Mavuso."

"I have something to say and you will listen to me," he demanded, grabbing her tighter and tugging her closer to him. With a force I had never seen in Khwezi, she swung her free arm and punched him square in the face. Mavuso staggered and she launched herself at him. I hesitated briefly, tempted to let her get in a few landing punches, then reached out and wrapped my arms around her waist, struggling to pull her away from him.

Mathembi came between us and Mavuso, whose bravado had returned, "Get out of my way Mathembi. Get out of my way!"

Khwezi screamed back, "I will kill you. Who the fuck do you think you are? How the fuck are you gonna grab me?"

Mathembi pleaded with Mavuso, "Baby, please," but he slipped out from behind her and advanced towards Khwezi, kicking the table and grunting like a bull. The table crashed over onto the floor, scattering broken bottles all over the room.

Khwezi wriggled from my grip and grabbed a half-broken bottle, brandishing it in Mavuso's direction, "If you touch me I will kill you!"

Suddenly, Mavuso's demeanour transformed entirely, his macho and domineering stance giving way to calm meekness. He was facing the door, so I turned to see what he was looking at. In the doorway stood our neighbour, an elderly man with a kind smile. He must have knocked unheard and opened the door in the commotion. Khwezi, who hadn't noticed our neighbour come in, was still shrieking, but Mavuso now faced the door and practically bowed. Calm. Like he never kicked over the table. Like he didn't just lug Khwezi across the room.

I watched the way the old man looked into the room, at the bottles on the floor and the one in Khwezi's hand. I saw it as he did, Khwezi huffing and puffing, livid and threatening to murder Mavuso. The younger man was calm in the midst of her threats. The neighbour must have thought that Khwezi kicked over the table.

Mavuso explained, "Angazi ukhuti ungenwe yini. But do not worry, I will take care of it."

The rest of us watched this moment, stunned and scared by Mavuso's shift. Mathembi sniffled in the corner. The older man nodded and left, believing Mavuso. As soon as we heard his apartment door shut, Mavuso growled at Mathembi, "Let's go!"

Mathembi lingered a moment, so he marched out the door leaving her behind.

She picked up her bag and I offered, "You can stay if you need to."

She shook her head and muttered a "sorry" to us all, wiping away her tears and gently closing the front door behind her. As soon as the door shut, Khwezi sat down and grabbed ice from the fallen ice bucket, applying it to her purple arm. Thato and Bassie moved about the room quietly picking and sweeping up the shattered glass. I sat down beside Khwezi and she rested her head on my shoulder. They slowly pieced together the apartment around us and only the silence and the now-wobbly table remained to remind us what just happened.

Stunned, nobody spoke until I said, "We need more alcohol."

All of us except Khwezi nodded in agreement and let out a tired laugh. Thato volunteered to go get it and Bassie left with her. We stayed behind and Khwezi proceeded to clean herself up quietly. Teetering with anger. I knew not to speak to her when she got this way. This was not the first time she had had to deal with men like this. Everywhere else, but not in our space, not like this.

She sat down and switched the TV back on. Noticing my stare, she just smiled at me. I poured myself a drink. Bassie and Thato returned and we drank, blasted music and tried to forget. Softly numbed by the alcohol, Thato pulled Khwezi into a dance and they jolled around the room. Forever the life of the party when they were together. I sat on my phone and played Sudoku, offering them a smile from time to time. When they finished dancing, Khwezi raised her eyebrows at me.

Her question: "Do you wanna be alone now?" I nodded back and she announced, "Okay guys, I think we can call it now, neh? I want to get jiggy with my lady."

Once we were alone, we climbed into the shower together and washed in silence. We climbed into bed, a small space between us as we looked at one another.

"This is not how I thought this night would end," she shared.

"Me, neither," I agreed, kissing her on the cheek and brushing fingers along her bruised wrist. She fell asleep quickly, leaving me shaken by the events of the night. I watched her sleep, crying softly so she wouldn't wake up and, finally, sleep came from the exhaustion of crying.

When I woke up, Khwezi was gone. I jumped out of bed and padded into the living room and then the kitchen, but she wasn't there. Her cell phone rang in the apartment when I called it, and I found it on the couch.

Panicked, I called Thato.

"No, I haven't seen her, but I will be there now and we can see how we look for her. I am sure she is okay."

By the time Thato arrived, I could feel a gnawing in my liver, kidneys or my heart, maybe all my internal organs slowly giving out from worry. As soon as I showed her Khwezi's phone, she headed into the kitchen and brought out a shot glass and vodka from the freezer.

"Khwezi would never leave her phone, Langa. Shit, man. Shit. Where do you think she is? Do you think she went to kill him? Do you think? Maybe she –"

Her thoughts were interrupted by the sound of heavy steps outside and shortly after, Khwezi entered, sweaty and jovial.

"Where the fuck have you been, bra?" questioned Thato.

"I went for a hike. Sorry." She walked over and smothered Thato in a hug. Thato squealed and shrugged her off. Khwezi turned to me but I shook my head, so she just sat across from me.

"What the hell, Khwezi?" I asked.

Not renowned for reading social cues, Thato picked up on my anger, announced she had a date with Bassie and left.

"Are you okay?" Khwezi asked once we were alone.

I didn't answer and she asked if I wanted to talk about last night. She was relieved when I said no, so she didn't push further, and apologised for leaving without telling me, citing my peaceful sleep as the reason.

I grunted and headed back to bed. Her audible sigh filled the room and she followed eventually. The bed sank as she settled in, and her eyes pierced the back of my head. She wanted my attention but knew how much I hated to be woken up so I heard her fidgeting until she eventually passed out. I noticed that this was the first time she had slept properly for the past week. Almost as if her body had been training her for this fight and now it was letting her rest.

This goes on for weeks. All she does is sleep. When she isn't sleeping, I catch her shaking when she watches TV or picks up the remote or every time the leg of the table gives in. When I want to talk, she doesn't, and when she does, I don't want to. I turn to my new therapist Charlie, and Khwezi drinks.

One night walking back home, it is a good night, a group of men walk towards us and we instinctively stiffen as we hear that laugh.

Mavuso makes a gesture and points at us and his posse erupts in laughter. We hear one of them say, "I can't believe you were ever friends with those people. They are crazy" as they cross the street before we pass them. Not letting me go, Khwezi picks up her pace.

When we get home, her father calls. He doesn't notice that she is upset so she doesn't say anything. I tell my mother about it and she comforts me, asks me if I want her to come, I say no. She asks how Khwezi is and I tell her she isn't fine, that she's not talking. She keeps quiet, wanting to say something reassuring, I know. There is banging from the kitchen and I tell uMama I have to go. Khwezi is banging the cupboard doors.

"What is it? What are you looking for?"

"My cup." She bangs another cupboard door shut. "I asked you not to move it from where I always put it."

"Khwezi, the cup broke that night. Remember? Thato was using it. They must have thrown it out when they were cleaning."

She stops moving and stares down at the counter.

"Listen, Khwezi. You need to talk to someone but you know better than to talk to me the way that you just did."

I move to stand behind her and wrap my arms gently around her waist. She tenses and I know she is thinking back to me holding her away from Mavuso.

"Do you want me to let go?"

She shakes her head no and turns around to look at me, keeping my arms around her waist. "I am really sorry about your cup, okay?" She is quiet and for the first time, she cries into my shoulder. We sit down and she talks and talks. As the days pass, and as she talks more, she no longer hides in her sleep.

⁘ ⁘ ⁘

I think everyone says the same thing about violent men. What else is there to say about them?

But we also hold hands here. In clubs, we grind and lamza one another without being completely afraid. We are hardly an anomaly. We are nothing worth staring at, even if there are those that do. I know a little freedom at UCKAR that is almost Makhanda.

But we still can't hold hands without some man or someone telling us "ngamanyala odwa eniwenzayo".

Grinding or kissing each other is an extreme sport. On the one hand, there are those spitting bile onto the floor beneath us, their burning disgust spewing out. There are, too, those that slither closer to us, trying to grind between us, whispering their desires and licking their lips: "We can make a plan between the three of us."

⁘ ⁘ ⁘

Once, when Khwezi's parents and sisters were away, we stayed at her place. Her home was precise and minimal: painted grey on the outside, a clinical white inside. Hedges and well-trimmed trees lined the driveway. No leaves littered the paving. I wondered if the trees were real and squinted against the sun, trying to peer through the glossy surfaces of dense foliage.

Khwezi chattered on, enthusiastic, at ease. I smiled at her quietly as we slid into the house. There was something about her parents' house that reminded me of public waiting rooms. Waiting in hospitals. Waiting in banks. Waiting in a queue, occasionally staring at other eyes glassy with boredom. Cold aircons, white walls, and only furniture with a functional purpose, that kind of waiting. I edged into the space carefully.

"You hungry?"

As we cooked together, music coloured her house a better mood. Her family's omnipresence wilted away with each thud and clunk of Khwezi chopping away and the loud hissing as vegetables were tossed into a pan on the stove. I felt less nervous about being there. The wine we shared buzzed away any anxiety I had left.

Having cleared the kitchen, popcorn ready, we settled into her bed to watch a movie. A boring one that had sounded promising. Khwezi was fidgeting beside me, the wine's heat tickling her loins. At least I thought so because my own blood felt warm with liquid courage.

We'd had sex before that night. Together, and with others before. With her a number of times in classrooms and public toilets, random locations that were the consequence of spontaneous desire and no privacy, the result of not owning property. Yet, it was different that night. And different would be an inadequate adjective to describe what I studied about hands that night. Hers and mine.

Tentative fingertips shivered across skin, tip-toeing paths of anticipation up and down backs. Softened strokes that tickled beneath underwear, turned steady and persistent as they ventured deeper. Palms patted apart limbs, landed saucily on thighs, behinds, made way for peeling, feeling, encountering.

Of course, every time you have sex, it will not be identical: moods, spaces, times, touches, intentions all drift and mingle, forming new pathways, reflecting and drawing from past journeys, and ending somewhere that may look similar. But isn't.

We'd had sex, laughing all the way through. Queef sex, "a love language". Awkward at times, limbs flying out wildly – "You accidently kicked me", "Are you okay?" – uncoordinated, uninhibited sex. That night, her palm rested on my cheek and mine on hers, fingers skimming along the moisture from one another's eyes.

Afterwards, snuggling into sleep, I whispered into the faintly lit room: "I wasn't crying. It was just my allergies."

Her amused breath warmed my ear as she responded, "Yah, and my eyes were reacting to the onions I chopped earlier."

"Yoh, girl, i-sex!"

✦ ✦ ✦

In the same year that I moved in with Khwezi, my mother decided to come along for what was still called the Grahamstown National Arts Festival. uMama liked comedy so that was one of the first performances she had decided to go and see. I invited Khwezi too and sat sandwiched between them, aware of and inhaling the difference in their fragrances, their moods. It was a responsive audience, lively and constantly cackling. The comedian on stage in the spotlight was sharp, focused, mocking.

"*I was at a cinema and the movie was getting very raunchy. You know one of those steamy scenes where you pray to the heavens you never have to date an actress.* [Cackle.] *And then all of a sudden, I could hear some moaning. I'm like 'Hayi, maan. I am sure it's just the movie.' But I could hear the sound was definitely coming from right behind me.* [Cackle.] *And I am mos very curious yabo. So ngajika vele. Yeeeeeyi. You wouldn't believe. Fingering. FI-NGE-RING!* [Cackle.] *Besides the fact that we were in a whole cinema guy; WHO? In 2018? Even fingers anymore?*" [Cackle. Cackle.]

Khwezi's hand curled around my wrist, squeezing. Tense. On my other side, my mother sat motionless, staring at the comedian, unblinking, biting her lip. I wondered whether she was thinking about Khwezi and I, and why she did not laugh.

✦ ✦ ✦

"*Eish, dude. Your knuckle is seriously hurting me, hey. Twist your hand that way instead. Yah. Yah, like that. Yah. Okay sharp, that's perfect. Hmmmm. Okay. Hmmmmm, mmmm. Ouch! Kanti what's happeniiiiing? Uzama ukukokoda lapho noma? Tuck those knuckles away, tu.*" [A pause. Some twisting.] "*Yaaaaaaaaaah. OOOOOOH! Yahhhhh!*"

LANGA: I'd like to get a dildo.

KHWEZI: A dildo?

[*Langa pauses, narrows her eyes thoughtfully, then shakes her head and lifts her lip on one side, before grinning.*]

LANGA: Noooooo! A strap-on.

KHWEZI: I mean I've never considered it but we could try it out. [*shrugs*] Let's check out how much it costs.

[*Online. Matilda's. Luvland. They look at each other quietly.*]

LANGA: Okay maybe we can save up and talk about this in a few months.

✦ ✦ ✦

There is so much. About her creases, the light, little intonations in her sighs. I discover that my skin can carry her, that I can know what she feels like without opening my legs, without closing my eyes, when I am walking down the street without touching her.

5
Together in Makhanda

A hasty turn of the lock before the door opens. I don't see anyone at the door but hear the rustle of shopping bags. Khwezi heaves them in and onto the kitchen table, booting the door closed behind her. Wonderful surprises poke out at me from the bags: Oreos, ice-cream and chicken wings from Spar because Makhanda still does not have a Chicken Licken and KFC never has wings. My eyes beam from the bags to her amused glance.

She pulls off her boots and places them by the door, her socks slide her across the room towards me. Before I can untangle from the warm blankets and the hot-water bottle to hug her, she dives onto the bed, her thighs in jeans on either side of me, pinning me down, clasping my face in her hands.

"Eh-eh. Yooooh," I push her palms away. "Why ungagqokanga ama-gloves?" She laughs, a conspiratorial chuckle.

I glare at her.

"I go out into the chilling, treacherous and unforgiving Makhanda cold for you and this is how you –" I hadn't detected her icy hands creeping sneakily under the blankets ...

"THANK ME?"

Her palms land on my heated breasts, knowing this is always the warmest part of my body and she squeezes as I yelp.

"Khwezi!"

A playful shove and she tumbles off the bed, staggering towards the kitchen.

Her Terminator voice: "I'll be back."

Our laughter collides at the centre of the room, bubbling up, melting into the walls.

"You'll get warm soon. The heater is on."

I watch her fill the kettle as I trudge across the room, a hot-water bottle wedged into my pants. We unpack the shopping bags and she saves one for last.

"Soooooo! I present to you –" A soaring arm and dramatic unpeeling of the plastic wrapping: "The Period Pain Package. PPP for short."

Her eyes shimmer with excitement and the adrenaline of performance. I laugh out loud. Her animated right hand swoops into the bag, pulls out the box of Oreos. Her left hand follows, revealing butter-flavoured microwave popcorn. Khwezi coos as she continues to unpack. The spicy aroma of the barbecued wings as she sets them on the tabletop. Finally, she beats out a drumroll on the tabletop, plunges both arms deep into the bag and, parodying exaggerated effort, hauls out the tub of Tin Roof dairy ice cream. A feast.

I laugh uncontrollably, circling the table to hug her.

Khwezi sheds her clothes as I reheat the kettle for tea and get the snacks ready. We binge-watch TV series, taking a day off from university and life.

Our shared reason: period pains. More than enough reason to stay home.

After supper, we play cards.

"So," Khwezi begins, masking her face coyly behind a spread of cards, "I thought we could try something."

"OooKay?"

The fanned spread in her hand slithers sneakily down to her nose. Her wide, innocent eyes light up with mischief above the pleats of the fan. Swiftly, Khwezi dumps the cards face-down on the bed, leaps up and darts into the kitchen. The apartment crackles as she rummages through that bag of goodies still on the table. A whisper of pink peeks out from behind her back as she walks towards me, keeping her surprise hidden.

Springing onto the bed, she yells, "Ta-da!"

I squint, uncertain, turning the box of condoms in my hands. "And now?"

Naughty and testing, her broad smile. Briefly, she reminds me of my small sister playing a dare-devil game.

"Weeeellll ... you said you were willing to try it out the other day."

I frown.

"Yes, you did. Remember when we read that article about all the benefits? Well, here we are." My eyes move down to the box and back to her.

"I don't know about this, yazi."

"I even got some spare towels," she encourages.

"Okay then," I nod, "We can try."

Peeling back the plastic wrapping, I pull out a thin condom as she leaves to get the towels. Remembering the reason for the towels, I slip into the bathroom, ripping off my bloody pad and rolling it into the bin. Wiping twice, I hope for a night's miraculous reprieve from bleeding despite the diluted red in the toilet bowl.

Khwezi has laid the towels out across the bed and is sitting there with a man's stretchy condom engulfing her hand. I burst out laughing.

"And what are you gonna do with that scary pink monster?"

She breaks into a noisy cackle. "I'm going to take her for a swim in the Red Sea."

My stomach hurts from laughter. I sit next to her, pressing palms against my belly, laughing still.

"We are not doing this. Angeke ngikhone."

Glancing at her hand again, "I can't take that thing seriously, yoooh!" Khwezi peels the latex off. It plops onto the floor, limp and flabby.

Eventually, our hilarity quietens down.

"It makes me uncomfortable because I want to but I don't know where to start. And I don't know how not to feel a little disgusted even though I know there's nothing wrong with it."

"I know. I was trying to make it a bit less like that for both of us."

Rubbing my fingers into the fleshy gaps between her plaits, I watch her curl into herself, her eyes\lids dipping low with pleasure. Standing up, I coo, "Would you maybe like some warm milk now?"

A small red dot winks at me from the edge of one of the towels. I tug it from the bed and sprint to the bathroom. Soaking it in cold water, I remember to replace my pad. Peeling off the flowery pink wrapper, I think about a young aunt of mine, the only person who had ever spoken to me about having sex during her period. She had been shocked, murmuring with disbelief how she had let her boyfriend run his tongue along her bloodied slit. Revulsion and thrill had wrangled in her eyes. Finally, a huge grin: "It was some of the best sex ever, mtshana!"

Saturday. The next morning.

Khwezi is still in bed, sleep lolling behind her eyelids. I slide across the bed, licking a path into the curl of her ear, nibbling softly at the lobe. She mumbles awake, moaning a good morning.

"Do you wanna join me in the shower?"

"Hmmmm. What's happening in the shower?"

Another ear-lick; my fingers beneath the soft silk of her pyjama shorts. Climbing out of the bed, into the bathroom, turning on the shower. The padded muffle of her footsteps following me.

Blood diluted pink in the pooled water at our feet, swirling before gurgling into the drain.

If my aunt and I were as close as we'd once been, I would have called to tell her I agreed with her.

Definitely, some of the best.

6
Knowing Khwezi, knowing myself

I try to keep a record of all the things I have learned about myself with Khwezi, being in bed together, in dark cinemas, on the kitchen floor with her. All I have learned about Khwezi. Because I know my memory can betray me, I scribble moments everywhere, impassioned notes on skin and breath.

It is a Bibliography.

- What she tastes like.
- What she smells like.
- Her smooth, abundantly moist skin.
- Breath: sharp, short, slow, tentative, all from different sources.
- Sounds.
- Silences.
- The coarse hairs and smooth ingrown marks on her vulva.
- Her welcoming vagina.
- That a vagina and a vulva are not the same things.
- That her clit and mine don't like the same things.
- That her vagina is quiet and broody.
- Sometimes Nkomazi. Sometimes a tang.
- Wet wipes are important.
- Crying is okay.
- Sex is okay. It is okay. It is nothing to be afraid of. It is nothing to be ashamed of.

After that first time we'd played "34 Questions for New Relationships", we decided to do it again every once in a while, to learn one another anew.

"What colour do you not like? Why? If it is attached to a memory, share this memory with your partner."

"I'll go first," Khwezi said.

When I was five, my parents bundled me and my older sister, Zenani, onto a bus with a couple of suitcases and many of our belongings left behind. They did not tell us where we were going or why we were in such a rush. We just left.

We arrived here at the home of Makazi Zinzi, my mother's sister, with whom we stayed for about a month until we could find our own place. Her cramped flat was musty and the walls cracked everywhere. I remember my mother scolded us about giggling and poking at the cockroaches that jived in those cracks.

When we finally moved from Makazi's place to where we live now, white was the colour of our new home. Grey outside. White inside. Not white like the stained off-white of my aunt's walls. But stark. Blinding. Stifling. Next to godliness. I don't like white, really. It reminds me what a flawed illusion that fresh new blank of a home was or became.

Holidays, we went back to Zimbabwe. To visit family, to eat all the good things we could not find here. To show your father's people that we are living well, my mum would say. Ambuya's house (the mother of my father) was a tower. Was towering. And quiet too. Silence circled and swathed itself around everything, even the three copper-red chickens that barely squawked. There was no TV, just the rolling empty distance from the nearest neighbours. Even the wind was careful with the trees, taking care not to get the leaves too excited. Only the small wild birds twittered on, morning and night, in response to our comments and questions, a soundtrack for our visit.

On the last trip we made to see Ambuya, my mother was pregnant with Kamva. We wouldn't be able to come back again because Kamva would not have a Zimbabwean passport. At least that's what my parents said, not why they couldn't just get her one. Ambuya looked exactly the same every year. I even think she bought many of the same outfits and just alternated between them as each tattered away from long use. The same chickens. And the house was also the same.

I was 10, though. And beginning to wonder and wander around by myself more often. A new family had moved onto a plot closer than the previous neighbours. A family of four, with two kids around my age. I heard them before I met them, breaking into the birds' songs with their naughty sing-song tunes.

Tendai, the daughter, came over to visit a few days before Christmas. The chickens had announced her arrival. From my bedroom window, I caught sight of her strutting towards the front door. I ran out to meet her.

"Ndiri Tendai," she said, small arms crossed, a sharp hip jutted outwards. Tendai was beautiful, more beautiful than anyone I'd ever seen. Of course, I'd only known 10 years of seeing people. But still. I wanted to crawl inside her and find out how someone the same age as me could be so strong and so mesmerising. We became friends, of course.

Inseparable. I can remember that holiday as if it happened yesterday, running around picking berries and chasing chickens. Her favourite game was hopscotch because she was so quick and nimble. That little grasshopper from next door, my dad would say. She would flounce around, her dress hopping along and fluttering up and down, her laughter singing in the wind.

I denied to myself what I was feeling. I knew about crushes. Even primary school kids know about crushes. But what I thought I knew was that crushes were little birds in cages reserved only for boys. I couldn't explain then why I felt like there was a flock of wild birds in my belly, their wings flapping enthusiastically every time I saw her. Or why those birds nested in my lungs, beaks snapping away all the air, leaving me winded and gasping. Why did I begin to dream about her?

Inseparable. Panting and huffing, we were lying in the tall, yellow grass beyond Ambuya's fence. A river hissed over stones not far from us. Berries the colour of blood stained our fingers and lips dark. Tendai had decided we should go gathering berries in this secret place, to lie cushioned and hidden by the grass. The sky was unimaginably blue, powder-white clouds dusted across it. I remember feeling so warm and so happy and not really knowing why. And then her blood-red lips were close to and on mine. It was a sweet kiss. Nervous, but tender. Everything Tendai tried not to reveal in herself.

We spent the rest of that day in that grass, breathing as one, inseparable.

When I arrived back home, my mother questioned.

— What's that on your lips Khwezi?

I had forgotten about the berry lipstick.

— I thought I told you not to eat berries from the bushes, heh? And what are you grinning about?

Although I knew I could have been smacked, the memory of the day I'd had dispelled any concern. I also knew that my mother was alone in the house. Everyone else had gone into town. She did not like to hit me herself, my mother. Instead, she would tell my father and the punishment would be left in his hands.

— Sorry, ma.

She was making chicken stew. Carrot and potato peelings were heaped in a neat hill on the table, scraps of slimy chicken stacked like a tree at the top. My grandmother's kitchen was small compared to the rest of the house.

Cramped. Cosy with bright checked plastic tablecloths and floral-all-over plastic mats. Ambuya liked flowers, went out to pick armfuls every Sunday morning. The blooms sat in vases in all the rooms. For the kitchen, she always picked yellow flowers to match the walls.

Adding the last dashes of salt to the stew, my mum sat down, asked for a cup of tea. Two sugars, no milk, a dash of cold water. I placed it in front of her. I was glad she had wanted the tea. It was the best time to speak to her when she was sipping something. And I was excited, bursting.

– Ma, how do you know if you love someone?

My mother doesn't smile often. At that moment, her eyes twinkled. She beamed.

– You just care a lot about them. You feel warm when you are with them. And they make you happy.

I sat at the opposite end of the table.

– But how do you know if you are happy?

– I don't know, Khwezi. You just know it (*her smile widening*). Why are you asking? Do you love somebody?

I was quiet. I was not sure if I did love Tendai. It didn't make sense to.

– Is it that neighbour's boy heh? You've been hanging around there a lot with that sister (*chuckling*). Have you been trying to get that little boy's attention?

I laughed. In a way my mother had warned me about. Heartily, the way she says girls in bars laugh. My stomach hurt, my face and throat felt hot.

– Uhleka ntoni, Khwezi?

– No, ma, it is not Tendai's brother. He is very silly and very boring and only cares about his toys. It is Tendai.

Te-Nda-Yi?

Immediately, I realised I should not have said anything, that I should not have told her. I should not have loved Tendai if that is what it was. Nor should I have kissed her. I should have saved my crush for her brother, as my mother had thought I was doing.

She rose and smacked me hard, releasing real not-berry blood in my mouth. The yellow room spun around and around in my dazed vision.

My mother was yelling.

— Te-Nda-Yi, Khwezi!!! Do you want to become a lesbian? Yintoni lento Khwezi?

I wished I had been what I should have been, felt what I was expected to feel, that I had been normal.

For the rest of the holiday my mother insisted I was sick. I couldn't go out to see Tendai. I couldn't go out even to hang underwear on the washing line. My mother made sure I remained in my bedroom, telling the whole family I had caught a virus of sorts from running about outside. It was contagious and they couldn't come in to see me.

I knew she had told my father the whole story though because one day I woke up to see him standing in the doorway, a pained and confused look on his face. I lay there looking at him, waiting for him to tell me it was fine and I could leave the room to go out and play. But he just stood there saying nothing, then left.

He was not the only one that came to my room. My mother invited the women from the local church, who came and sat around my bed, cloaked in starched robes that emulated the whiteness of the heavens. They also knew the truth, I could tell. My mother would lie to family, but she would not lie to the church. For a week, they came and adopted the same positions in the same chairs. I had come to know which woman would sit where: the scrawny, raspy one at the end of the bed at my feet, Miriam, with a bosom that could serve as a shelf, seated beside my right ear.

One woman named Dora—I learned their names as they spoke to one another—seemed exceptionally passionate about the evil they had come to eradicate. She would jump to her feet and scream out:

— Holy Ghost Fiiiiyyaaaaa! Remove this smear, this curse, the demons of this world from this child! Cleanse her, hallelujah!

For hours she would flit and dart back and forth around the room, warning her companions that this scourge would spread if not taken care of. They had to remove it before it destroyed God's people. Before it became the plague. Anyone who didn't know that this woman's headscarf swivelling, white robes flying, bony fingers pointing, and shrieking were all in the name of exorcising me would have thought her a possessed banshee. It took all my willpower not to laugh out loud sometimes.

Through all this my mother would remain seated on the floor in the corner of the room, shadowed and in mourning. As they left, the church ladies would make soothing noises:

— So sorry for what you are going through.
— How could this have happened?
— How could she do this to you, this child?
— Do not worry my sister, God will deliver her.

Maybe they were consoling themselves, relieved that their children did not do homosexuality to them. Some of them spoke in Shona, knowing my mother would not understand: "Zvakaoma".

On the last day they came around, the day before we were to return to South Africa, they brought me a white garment like a hospital gown and told me to put it on. Huddling me out of the room in a circle—me at the centre—they led me out of the house for the first time in weeks. I thought that they were containing my illness by stifling me that way, protecting my family. I also thought that we probably looked like a flower, them as petals, myself the centrifugal centre.

We walked out that way, sometimes stumbling over one another's bare feet, an undignified waddle. Outside I remember the world looked so new, so absolutely amazing. Like the day I'd first worn prescription glasses and everything was suddenly clearer. The sky was the same blue as the day I'd last seen Tendai, and between the gaps of the white robes, and from the distant breathing of water, I knew we were close to the spot where we'd kissed.

We arrived at a not-too-deep river. My petals fell from me, scattered around the riverbank. My mother was there, also in white, a bible clasped in her hand.

— Ma?

Stoic as the statue of Joan of Arc, an angel in stone.

Thick hands roped around my arms pushing me further down the riverbank. Water tickled my feet, slippery in between each toe. Sharp stones dug and scratched the soles of my feet as they shoved me deeper into the river and I resisted, all the while calling for my mother who only stood there and watched. I thought of the story of Mary Magdalene, wondered if this is how she had been jostled and lugged about by the crowd for being a harlot. Would my mother now throw stones at me? Would these women of the church join her, punish me for my sin? Would I see the white-white of their cloaks when the stones finally smashed the light out of me? Or only hell fiya? When would Jesus come? Would He tell them to cast the first stone only if they had not sinned, save me as he had saved Mary Magdalene? And where were my fathers now? The one I continued to pray to and the one I looked like.

I fell into the water, wet leaves sticking to my dress. Rushing water over my head, relentless, deep and flowing fast.

— I am sorry, ma. I am sorry. I am sorry.

Hands pulled me up as I spluttered and spat out river water. Paper bristled as my mother swiped past pages of scripture. I felt palms on my back, some hands pressing on my collarbone as I stood there trapped in the river looking up at my mother, a white figure encircled by the sun, doing the work of God.

They dunked me under, repeatedly. She began to read aloud.

– Do not have sexual relations with a man as one does with a woman; that is detestable ... (*dunk*). Do not defile yourselves in any of these ways (*dunk*) ... Everyone who does any of these detestable things–such persons must be cut off from their people. DO NOT HAVE SEXUAL RELATIONS WITH A MAN AS ONE DOES WITH A WOMAN ...

Do not. Do not. Do not.

I never saw Tendai again.

I never told my mother I still desired women, loved them. She wouldn't bother praying for me a second time. I did not want to be cut off from my people.

✦ ✦ ✦

Khwezi told me that even after all these years, her mother still asks her often, with disgust, mockingly, "Do you still think you are gay like you did when you were ten years old?"

✦ ✦ ✦

"Yellow."

"My favourite colour is yellow," I shared.

"My mother hates the colour yellow."

"Okay."

"Sorry."

.... silence ....

Again. "Sorry. What I should have said is 'Why is that so?'"

I smiled: "That's okay. And I don't know. I guess not many things remind me of light."

A question crept into her, lighting up her eyes: "Why's that?"

"Why is what?"

"Why do few things remind you of light?"

I ignored her curiosity. "Your favourite is blue, right?"

She smiled, "You remembered."

Blue reminds me of ghosts, I thought. Said nothing.

Instead, I asked: "How come?"

⁂

Often, we fight about our parents. Like them. The way they fought. In their name. Defending them against one another.

Khwezi accuses me of demonising her parents, making them out to be villains, begs that I give them a second chance, look past their mistakes. I push her away, afraid of all the reasons I think she would leave me.

Often after we fight I dream about the ocean, raging and beautiful. A blue that burns itself into my mind. My parents hover above it, pale and fading.

uMama screaming, "Uyinja! Hamba uba uyahamba! I hope uginywa yitsunami kulokaka ye-Durban."

And my father would be gone, his voice ebbing away in the water, in blue tides. Somehow in this dream, I know that blue was, may still be, his favourite colour. Wherever he may be.

I want to drink every morning after I have this dream, after we fight. I do drink. I must wipe it away and blot it out, the dream, the fear that this is our last fight.

Khwezi suggests I go to therapy. She is scared I will become an alcoholic, if I am not one already. I am afraid too. I start seeing Charlie, a therapist with the university Student Health Clinic.

⁂

Maybe we are a lie, Charlie, I tell him. We lie about being together. We are nothing more than "friends" to her family. I lie about how happy I am even when I am tired of not existing. To her, I lie. What do I expect? I knew I would be a secret. But I didn't think being a secret would be this exhausting. I didn't know we would have to become a pair of liars.

7
What is unremembered

Black. Absolute darkness.

"That's all you can recall?" Charlie probes.

Yes. It was some day, some weekend. I can't really remember which one even though I can recall other uncanny details. I spent most of my weekends visiting my grandparents back then. Someone – my grandma or grandpa, or my aunts who lived in the spare rooms outside – gave me some money and told me to go to the shop. I was wearing a white Nike tennis skirt that rustled when I walked, with a peach t-shirt that also had the statement "swoosh" on the front. Wind blew the dust into little hurricanes that raced one another down the street before spinning to slow stops like the game ama-top which my cousin and I used to play in that same sandy street together.

Across the road, uChris sat in the shadow of his vending stall, packets of chips and sweets hanging all around in rows and squares of bright colours. He smiled at me and waved as I opened the gate. Discomfort blew goosebumps down the skin on my legs. I tugged at the skirt. I waved back. We were usually not allowed to go to Mavis' tavern. I did that day. Did I go there because my grandfather was the one who'd sent me to buy him his evening bottle of Castle beer? He hadn't sent me out before, but I was getting older and Mavis would know the beers were for him. Or did I go there because it was windy and the streetlights were coming up for the night and the other spaza shops were further away? This is another thing I don't remember.

Whatever the reason, I found myself in the gloom of the tavern, on the side where they ran the spaza. This room was a small box, framed and guarded on three sides by steel bars. Behind the bars were fridges and shelves stacked with a variety of goods and what would be the fourth wall was the entrance.

There was a man in a striped navy and white t-shirt in front of me, buying something, cigarettes maybe. He stuck his hand through the bars to retrieve his purchase and disappeared into the twilight.

"Ngiyabuya manje," said the person behind the counter in response to a shouted request, disappearing into the tavern behind them.

I hadn't heard anyone come in behind me until uChris' voice trailed down my back, "Langa".

I can remember my back pressing into the bars behind me and my skirt lifted, riding up my thighs. His stroking along them and in between. And then.

"Black. Absolute darkness."

"That's all you can recall?"

"Yes. That's all."

My therapist, Charlie, pursed his lips.

I asked: "Do you think it happened?"

Pushing the stubby tips of his fingers against one another.

"It's possible."

My eyes searched for answers in his. His gaze avoided mine.

"It could be a distorted memory, fragments taken from television or other things you've watched, from dreams even."

I ground my teeth, slightly irritated that he would think this was just a figment of my imagination. Yet I could feel a seed growing in me, an idea sprouting, ready to erase this, to throw it into the "just your imagination" Pikitup bin in my head.

"Or" – I should have detected the "but" in his tone, I thought, as he continued – "it could be real. Sometimes your brain represses moments it doesn't want to remember. Traumatic ones. It can leave you with pieces of that memory floating around, disconnected, or it can leave you completely unable to recall anything. Like dreams."

His words reverberated in my head, bouncing around in the darkness there. Colours exploded in a headache behind my eyes, flickering so fast and vividly I had to close them. The white skirt my mother gave me. Red, pink, yellow lollipops. Amashwashwam nama kip-kip. I whirled up from my armchair, forcing open my eyelids to look at the clock.

"Time's up!" Grabbing my purple sling bag from beside the chair, I moved to the door, pinning my gaze on the detailed carving on its gold handle. I'd never noticed the intricacy before.

"Thank you, Charlie. I'll see you next week."

The walk home felt like a bubble of melting colours with me floating in its centre. Khwezi was in "writing mode" when I got home. Knowing she wouldn't want me to interrupt her, I stripped naked and climbed into bed, lay there staring at the wall.

The clicking of her keyboard stopped. "Don't you have a lecture after lunch?"

Swaddling myself tighter in the blankets: "I'm not going."

Hesitation. Fingers hovering over her keyboard. Her laptop smacked shut. She loped across the room and climbed onto the bed behind me, knotting her limbs through the spaces between mine.

"Do you want to talk about it?"

"Not right now."

She nodded.

✦ ✦ ✦

The following week.

"I'm ready to talk about it, Charlie."

He let his head tilt to one side, raising his left brow in a question mark.

"Seriously," I insisted.

He looked like he spent his life sitting in the sun, I thought to myself. Like peanut butter. With eyes the blue-green of the ocean.

Khwezi chuckled when I told her how handsome I thought Charlie was. "You and these mkhulus."

"I actually wanted to ask you something ... How are your relationships with men?"

Men? What kind of a question was this?

"Fine. My relationships are fine." I glared at him. "What does that have to do with what I told you last week?"

He slid his hands down the arms of his chair, tapping against the wood.

"I'm just thinking ... you never speak about any men. Not many friends, family. Your father?"

I wanted to tell him that he was being typical, believing that all my problems revolved around men. That I had daddy issues. Or heart-wrenching experiences with men that led me to like women. That I was a woman and couldn't exist without a penis.

"What does my father have to do with possibly being raped or molested, Charlie?"

I could hear myself sounding defensive but, fuck, he was pissing me off.

"All I'm saying is ..."

"No, Charlie. There's no point talking about people who leave, like my father. And I have friends. They just happen to be women."

He was quiet.

"I have no problem with men. I just have a problem with men who feel entitled to women. And that just happens to be so many of you."

⁂

uMama also thinks I am gay because my father was not around. She told me this, said that I don't know what good men that stay look like. I almost asked her if she did, if she knew good men who stay. Why was she still alone then? Instead, I told her I have all the people I will ever need in her. A truth I must always remember.

⁂

There are three weeks that I remember my dad most clearly. Those weeks before everything in my world became very noisy, came crashing down, everything colliding, falling apart. My mother's birthday. She was 33 and I was 10 years old. We threw a party for her. My dad had spent the first week of July buying gold balloons and streamers, huge silver letter 3s, hauling them home with him in the taxi. One day it was packets of chips and sweets in abundance and, on that first Friday, he and his friends had come in laughing, hoisting crates of spirits.

Each time he walked into the house with more party goods, the mood in the house lifted. Xola was three years old then. When nobody was watching, I stole sweets for her and myself. uMama was smiling all that week and she kissed him thank you. We were all happy.

On the first Sunday, uMama, Xola and I went to church without my dad – he said his church was in his heart – and when the priest called for us to kneel on our leather prayer pillows and give thanks, she praised the efforts of her husband in making her happy. I copied her, thankful to have the best dad who loved me so much.

We came back to a quiet house that Sunday. He was not watching soccer on TV with a beer in his hand the way he usually was on Sundays. And the house did not smell faintly of cigarettes he had tried to air out because my mother hated his habit. The house was quiet and it smelled like nothing at all. Empty.

I remember that I asked my mother where he was.

"I don't know", she said. "He will be back later. "

Her only response, repeated for the next week he was gone.

The party goods sat in the living room corner. Xola and I continued to pick at the sweets. On the second Sunday, the three of us went to church. uMama was silent during the prayer. I asked for my dad to be safe because I loved him.

When we walked into the house, the radio, not the TV, was on. Metro FM, my mother's favourite. The house did not smell like cigarettes and there was a fast-food packet on the counter. Xola and I rushed screeching into the living room to find him sitting, reading a newspaper. When he saw us, he rose and bundled us each under an arm. I still remember the smell of him that day. uMama stayed in the kitchen.

We giggled and writhed in his arms as he carried us into the kitchen. She stood still, blankly staring at the food on the counter. He put us down and moved towards her. She did not respond when he called her, nor when he placed his hand on her waist. She cried when he pulled her into him. I remember feeling so happy that my parents loved each other so much. And being so happy that my dad was fine.

That last week before the party, we were happy again. Except uMama did not smile nor kiss him. She was a little angry at him, but we were fine. Except that then I heard her whisper-shouting at him as I was brushing my teeth.

"Durban! Durban! Awundiqheli kakubi? Already you were gone for how long, now you want to be gone to Durban?"

I could make out the deep mumble of his response, but not what he said to her.

"Yazi yintoni inxaki?"

There was no response. She continued, "Uyinja! Hamba uba uyahamba!"

I heard shuffling in the room, the whine of the old wardrobe door, followed by a thud on the floor. I moved to stand just outside the bathroom, desperate to see more than the sheen of uMama's nightdress through the small gap in the door.

My father's tone sharpened. Stabbing but still quiet. I could picture the small spittle string that always escaped through his teeth when he was mad. My face felt slightly hot imagining his breath, but also panicked by overhearing this first fight between my parents. A long silence hung in the darkness following the words I did not hear and the rattle of keys made it sink deeper into my stomach. I felt like I was watching myself watching the door. Yet I did not blink, nor jump when it swung back, knowing I would be in trouble for eavesdropping.

We stood gaping at one another, a startled and then determined look on his face. A toothbrush hanging from my lips.

"I am going to get a beer, Langa."

A beer, with a travel bag in his hand?

"I hope uginywa yitsunami kulokaka ye-Durban!" my mother shouted from inside the room.

"Okay," I said.

✦ ✦ ✦

Sometimes I think therapy is so stupid. People are dying or whatever and I choose to sit with a white man telling him how broken I think I am. What am I doing, vele? How dare I waste my mother's money?

✦ ✦ ✦

Why would my father say: "I am going to get a beer, Langa"?

✦ ✦ ✦

The people we knew before one another. The boys we let fondle us. Dry-humping. The anticipation of our first kisses. Hiding notes in classes. Wet dreams. The first penis I saw face-to-face, peeing in the street, how it chased me down the street, a dangling predator.

Mosesane. I told Khwezi that I didn't tell my family about uChris. Because I didn't know if I was lying to myself. Because why must you cause more pain to others over a loss you can't remember? How does anyone begin to explain how "nothing" looks?

"Is that why you don't talk about your father? Because you can't remember him leaving you?"

I can't remember him at all, I tell her. You can't feel pain over someone when you remember nothing about them.

8
Mosesane

In a pool. At a party.

Mosesane and I met there for the first time. He dared me to jump in, thinking I would strip to my underwear. Instead, I dove in wearing my jeans. Standing above me on the brick paving, he said, "You're a little crazy aren't you?"

"A rollercoaster," I dared.

He told me that was exactly what he was looking for.

We went home together. His home at least. For months we went to his home. Never mine. I stopped going there when he told me I had commitment issues.

✧ ✧ ✧

"We just kissed, I swear."

✧ ✧ ✧

Mosesane was one of the ghosts that came to visit when Khwezi and I moved in together. I didn't tell her, but I dreamed about him a lot. Sometimes I dreamed I was standing in an ocean watching the waves rise into mountains, looming high overhead. In the distance I could glimpse the dots of swimmers' heads out in the ocean and among them Mosesane, waving and daring me to swim out to him. Sometimes I woke up after swimming all the way out there, feeling the warmth of holding his wet body and treading water. In other dreams, I struggled awake just as the water closed over his head. I wondered how different we would have been together – he and I – if I had met him after I met her. After all, being with her taught me trust.

If I'd met Khwezi before I met him, on the other hand, my relationship with her would also have been different. In the six months I spent staying over in Mosesane's home, nights together watching documentaries, sprawled naked in his bed, talking Neo-Soul or laughing at Bob's Burgers, he taught me how to glory in my nakedness. And that intimacy can be lovely, a warm place you don't need to be afraid to stay within.

⁂

Mosesane had a way of knowing to contact me just when I was set to visit Jo'burg. At times, I wondered if he stalked my university's academic calendar, but brushed it off as coincidence. As usual, I got a text from him during the mid-year vac in second year, suggesting we should grab a drink or hang out. We set up a day and time, met at a bar in the CBD.

"You chose a Wednesday of all days?" he greeted, gesturing to the dead bar, and rolling his eyes.

I smiled softly, rising to hug him. We sat back down. He ordered the same drink as mine, and I requested another.

"You know how to make an entrance, as usual," I teased when our waiter left with the order, "Still full of yourself."

Mosesane laughed nonchalantly, his eyes roving over my face and pausing at my lips. Noticing this, I announced, "You'll never guess which favourite commitment-phobe of yours is still going strong in her relationship."

His gaze moved from my eyes to my lips. I watched him roll his thoughts over in his head, weighing his response.

He chose his words carefully. "Hmmmm. Okay. Same person as before?"

I nodded, "Yup."

The speakers were playing a light rock tune, and we sat in silence listening to it. Thankfully, the waiter returned with our drinks, slightly lifting the awkwardness.

"So," I probed, "How have things been with you?"

A couple of beers and some five shots later, we staggered out into the night. When I'd suggested that I would get a cab home, he'd brushed me off and offered me a lift. So I followed him as he tried to remember where he had parked his car. It was a cool evening, not humid as Jo'burg could be, not as chilly as it could get at that time of year.

The streets were quite empty so we walked in the centre, tracing our steps along the dotted line. He was ahead of me, so tall it seemed his head was grazing the sky. I was too busy watching it among the stars that his sudden turn caught me off guard and I walked right into him. He, too, was knocked off balance by the impact and we tumbled onto the ground.

Our laughter echoed in the road as we lay there side-by-side. Remembering where we were lying, he jumped up and offered me his hand, pulling me right up against him. I stepped back slightly, clearly so he would notice me, turning my head this way and that as I dusted dirt off my body.

"How come we never got together? Like actually dating together? Even though we just get each other so well?"

My hand paused in its dusting and I lifted my head to look at him, caught off-guard by his question. From our new position, the moon was a halo behind his head.

"Remember," I said, "You said I was a rollercoaster and you were just in it for the ride. We both agreed to let things stay casual."

Mosesane pondered aloud: "And what if I regret saying we should stay that way?"

"Uhm ... Well. But I am seeing someone."

"I know that but –" He stepped in closer to me.

"No buts," I retorted, shaking my head.

Mosesane reached his hand behind my head, and I stopped shaking it. I felt rooted to the spot and when I did not move, he kissed me. Somehow he knew I'd let him.

⁂

It is baffling. I lie every day about the biggest part of my life, for Khwezi. Yet I could not lie to her about this. Not to Khwezi. I confessed.

"We just kissed, I swear."

She broke up with me. But we went on living together. With a co-signed lease that both our parents were paying off, Khwezi couldn't leave me unless she wanted to explain to her parents why we weren't able to go on sharing a place anymore. So she forgave me.

⁂

"Why did you kiss him?"

She hadn't spoken to me for over a week. On the first night after I told her about the kiss, her friend Thato slept over, slept between us in our bed. All three of us had watched *Come Dine With Me* earlier that evening, Thato laughing exuberantly and trying to nudge a conversation along. I muttered responses in a meek undertone. Khwezi spoke to Thato as if I wasn't there, laughing heartily with her friend. On the screen, the winner flaunted her prize money.

"I'm going to bed now, Thato. Goodnight."

Thato crept into the bed between us. I could hear their soft breathing, Khwezi pretending to sleep, Thato careful of her presence, taking in a few audibly sharp uncertain breaths before chirping, "Goodnight, Khwezi. Goodnight, Langa."

I woke up late the following morning. For a moment right after waking, I lay enfolded in that bright small space where everything is new. For that moment, Khwezi and I were okay. I lay still, my whole body wrapped in a blanket cocoon.

A thread of light crept in above my head. I could hear the dim rumble of a truck from the street below. Monday: a pick-it-up truck. The day was slowly creeping into my dark cave. Now I could smell eggs and toast. Coffee. The hibiscus tea a friend had given me. I poked my head out, light blinding me briefly. Thato was gone. Khwezi beckoned me towards the kitchen.

"Breakfast?"

I pushed on my slippers, loping towards her and seating myself on the stool next to her. We ate quietly, only the sounds of our chewing and slurping across the table. I heard her pause; the pull of saliva as she opened and then shut her mouth. But she said nothing.

"Yes, Khwezi?"

⁂

"Why did you kiss him?"

I don't know what I had expected. Not that question. It weighed down the room.

⁂

"What do you mean?"

"I mean, 'Why. Did. You. Kiss. Him?'"

I could hear all the "Fucks" in her tone. What she wanted to ask was WHY I FUCKEN KISSED HIM. She wanted to know how I could fucken do that? This is fucked up. You're fucked. Did you fuck him? Did you *want* to fuck him. That's what she wanted to know. Instead, she was asking me something I could not answer. Why had I let him kiss me?

I shook my head. We ate in silence. Another pause.

"I think we should see other people, Langa."

I gulped the tea down too quickly and heat scalded my tongue: "Yeah?"

She shook her head.

"You kissed him because you wanted to, no?"

"No."

"No?"

"Khwezi, I told you. He kissed me."

Her arched eyebrow threatened to disappear right up into her hairline.

"I think you wanted to kiss him. You wanted him. And maybe you wanted to do other things, also. Now I am giving you a chance ... Now you can stop being a fucken Golden Lesbian."

It wasn't funny. I did laugh though: "U-serious?"

"After all this time, we're going to go back to this again, vele?"

"I just think we should see other people so you can –"

"So I can go satisfy my bisexual desires for penises, angithi?"

"Angithi?"

She shrugged and slurped her coffee: you said it.

✦ ✦ ✦

One ground rule was established: anything we did with anyone else could not come into the apartment. No talking about them. No bringing them over.

✦ ✦ ✦

It was weird. Being together but apart.

✦ ✦ ✦

The day I first saw Langa was a slow-moving day. My mother had been quiet that morning, quieter than usual. Staring down thoughtfully into her black tea. Lots—which is what father let me call him—had gone off as usual in the morning. We would see him later. The kitchen was silent except for the chugging of the fridge and plip-plip of the leaking tap. Lots had been promising for weeks to fix it.

— Molo, Mother.

She grunted an uninterested response.

I pulled out a brown loaf and put peanut butter and jam on the table, set about spreading slices for breakfast and a packed lunch. The soft plop of butter and jam joined the plip-plip.

— Is everything okay?

Plip. Plip. Plip. Mother's head nodded so slightly I almost missed it. I nodded back cautiously.

— Okay.

Lunch packed into my schoolbag, I slid out of the front door, calling out: — Goodbye.

By sixth period in class, I found myself looking down at open books from the same dazed distance, words on the pages and spoken around me blurring together into a pool as dark as black tea. Not only was it a hot day, it was slow-moving, and time dragged, sweat pooling on the back of my neck and between my thighs. A stokvel of birds agitated outside the window, their stick-legs crossed as they gossiped in high clucks, pecking with excitement at the breadcrumbs scattered from people's lunches. What a time they were having.

— Khwezi?

— Yes?

Forty-six eyeballs were focused on me. A few sniggers hung about before dissipating under Ms Gunner's glare.

— Do you have anything to say about Langa's question?

I could feel my eyes widen with nervous surprise and embarrassment. Mother always teased me that my eyes widened round like the full moon when I was scared, or lying. The birds cackled, the fat one I'd named Madam Chair flapping her wings in a huff.

– There is no Langa in the class, ma'am.

Bursts of laughter. My moon eyes swivelled around, looking for support, any allies in the class, wordlessly begging for somebody to help dig me out of whatever hole I'd just buried myself in. Ms Gunner squinted down at me, amusement and annoyance vying in her blue eyes.

From behind me, a steady voice asserted: – I'm the Langa.

A fresh bubble of laughter popped and exploded into the unmoving heat, hot tears of shrill amusement dripping down to join the sweat. Even Ms Gunner covered her mouth with one hand, her body shaking with suppressed mirth.

I whirled in my seat, spun around, long braids smacking the girl in front–thwaaa! The class was now dissolving into a puddle of their own sweat and tears of laughter. Here was a girl I had never seen before: short bob-dreads, a hint of eyeliner circling eyes that were not wet with laughter like everyone else's. Eyes that seemed to be both empty and full, the edge of the horizon at nightfall.

She smirked slightly, the Langa girl.

– Hi. I'm new.

When she smiled, that's how we began. I fell into her eyes.

✦ ✦ ✦

At first, Khwezi would come home chuckling, more to herself than to me: "It was so weird today. I tried to chat up a girl from my lectures."

I gave an uncertain laugh, soft to mask my surprise. I didn't think she was serious about seeing other people. She hadn't done anything, at least nothing that I knew about, since she'd brought up the idea of seeing other people.

"Uh-huh?"

She scratched her neck. I knew she was uncomfortable.

"It was weird going up to her. But to top it all off she asked me about you, how you were doing?"

Oh.

"It seems I'll have to work harder to convince people we're not together."

⁂

Then there was a girl. In a club. With Khwezi. And when Khwezi saw me and knew I was watching them together, she kissed the girl. From then on there were others.

⁂

When we'd agreed to keep our apartment a neutral space, I'd thought it would be better, less painful. But the silence taunted me. It created distorted images in my head of what Khwezi was up to. Even playing the TV loudly, I could not drown out how lonely I was in that apartment. I ignored the texts Charlie sent to find out how I was doing when I missed one, then two, therapy appointments.

For the first time ever, I called my mother and cried on the phone. When she asked me what I had done, I said nothing. She asked me if it was over and I said, yes. I don't know if she sighed because she was happy or because she didn't know what more to say.

Almost as though crying to my mother was the thing I needed to shake me back into myself, I decided to let it be. Khwezi had made her decision and I just had to live with that.

The three clubs in Grahamstown were handy for meeting people. Oldies was packed with hip-hop skrr skrrs jamming to aspiring rappers and singers. I'd gone out with a random bunch of students I knew from lectures, and we'd ended up separated within the crowd, my classmates' faces hard to pick out through the smoke in the room. Not only did it smell acrid from cigarette stubs put out on the floors, there were sweetish traces of smoked joints and the mustiness of too many jumping bodies squeezed up against one another. I couldn't breathe and slipped out onto the pavement outside, the bell on the door chiming behind me.

A gust of cold air smacked me as I stepped out, knocking me about, peeling away the warmth from inside. A few students were scattered around the street, some obviously drunk, others brandishing packets of fast food. I watched the mist from my mouth spiral white into darkness. Behind me, the bell announced the door opening.

"Hey. Are you okay?"

I turned to see a woman just slightly taller than me, pulling her grey hoodie close. She was smiling slightly, a small smile that you had to be careful to notice. I nodded an answer to her question. I thought she was quite cute, in an "I'd like to make you my rebound" kind of way.

So, after thirty minutes of standing in the cold, my lips starting to numb, shivering, I gave her my number. She didn't ask for it. I realised that Khwezi was right when she said, "It was weird." But it was now necessary.

✦ ✦ ✦

Our first date. At a coffee shop. Seated outside, beneath an olive tree.

The wooden table and chairs were slightly rickety, but the old, worn conversation they made as they scraped against the floor suited the kindness of the room. It felt like somebody's home. This made me more comfortable.

We'd hung out a couple of times, having run into each other with mutual friends and acquaintances. Once in her res room when she invited me to listen to some of the music she made, we'd kissed. I hadn't been on a first date since my first date with Khwezi, so I was slightly anxious.

It didn't help now that she was late.

Leaves scattered onto the table. One drifted onto my shoulder, so delicately one would have thought it was placed there. I plucked it off and held it by the stem, fascinated by the strength of an old memory of falling jacaranda blossoms, a memory created long ago and as vivid as ever. I was so focused on remembering that I did not see someone walk towards me.

"Hello."

I looked up. Khwezi's face looked back at me.

"Hi."

Behind her, the other woman walked in, paused and glanced about in search of me. When she noticed me, she smiled, that same tentative smile from before. I waved to her and she walked towards us.

"Hey," she greeted Khwezi, extending her hand. That seemed so formal, so final a gesture, as if she was declaring her existence in my life.

Khwezi squinted hard at me before shaking the woman's hand.

"This is Khwezi." I introduced them. "Khwezi, this is, uhm ... this is ..."

"Keamo."

They stood there, hands still clasped, both looking at me.

"Order #31." A call drifted out from inside the coffee shop.

Letting go of Keamo's hand, Khwezi shoved her hand into her pocket and glanced down at her receipt. She waved the receipt and muttered the number.

"Okay, then. I guess I will see you later," she nodded. Adding "At home," before retreating into the interior.

I stood there watching her, knowing that Keamo was looking at me, was slightly confused about why I would not look back at her. I thought I must have looked nutty, frozen, a bit cooked, just standing there. I'm not sure how long I stood there, no longer really looking at anything. Not Khwezi. But just lost in something I couldn't understand.

"Langa!"

My body was shaking violently. I couldn't make it stop.

"Langa!"

Oh ... it was just Keamo. I hadn't noticed her move to stand in front of me, hands on my shoulders. Trying to get me to calm down, I guess. She really was cute, even more so with all that concern on her face. Like those cute dogs on Instagram who try to make their owners happy/ier. I could see her concern morphing into panic, her eyes growing a little bit wider, her mouth opening and closing, opening and closing.

"It's okay," I managed, the words coming from somewhere new, an alien place. "Ngi-right."

The panic was now disbelief, surprise even. I pulled her hands from my shoulders and moved back onto my chair, which squeaked its falsetto tune beneath me. Keamo followed me slowly, never not looking at me, almost as if she were scared I would crumble into ashes and blow away if she moved too quickly. Finally, the creak of her own chair joined mine in its song.

To rest the many questions in her eyes, I repeated, "Ngi-right, Keamo."

Twilights here are beautiful, perhaps the most beautiful thing in the town. The sky playfully swims from light, dusty lavenders to endless oranges and reds. And when you're lucky, you glimpse the deep velvet of night edging in, and with it the slight glimmer of stars. This was the marvel all about me as I walked home; the whole town a dream purple one moment and hot and on fire the next.

To my surprise, the light was on when I arrived at the apartment and from outside the door, I heard the sizzle of food cooking and the glossy murmur of a TV ad. Khwezi was home. For once. Cooking, even. When I walked in she was sitting at the kitchen table, pretending to look at something on her phone. I knew she'd heard me creak up the staircase.

"Hi," I greeted her, pulling off my jacket and shoes and searching for my slippers.

"Unendzara?"

I had learned enough Shona from hearing Khwezi speak to her father that I knew she was offering me food. I stopped fidgeting.

Number 1: She was offering me food.

Number 2: She was offering me food in Shona. She refused to speak Shona with me when she was really mad. It was like she thought, "You're an idiot so you only deserve English."

Number 3: She was home, cooking, not sitting with her headset on, offering me food. In Shona.

"Kwenzakalani, Khwezi?"

Without an answer, she rose and began to dish up beef stew and rice, vegetables that reminded me of Sundays at home. I watched her quietly, waiting for the end of her dramatic pause. She didn't speak, only placed the two meals next to one another at the table, poured out two glasses of juice and settled down again. I allowed myself to be beckoned forward; sat down.

We ate without speaking, quietly, remembering how we hadn't been quiet and together in three months.

She confesses.

I don't tell her I was too. Jealous, that is.

"I'm sorry for everything," she says.

"Me too," I respond/I lie/I guess. I am not too sure how I feel. I was only just beginning to get used to being separate.

✦ ✦ ✦

There were no more "other girls".

The rule remained: we did not talk about them.

9
#RUReference List

We'd known before. That Rhodes University, as it was still called then, was small and people slept around. That many of them didn't really use condoms. That our pharmacies ran out of morning-after pills sometimes. That drunken sex was everyday. That we believed the idea that when you sleep with someone, you sleep with all the people they've slept with. If we believed that idea, more than half of us students had slept with each other. That sex is part of the culture; protected or otherwise.

That is why people went crazy when the stories were revealed on the UCKAR Facebook page. Somebody – whose account was later identified as being false – confessed that they were HIV-positive and that they had slept with other students without a condom, while knowing their status. Social media was in an uproar: people telling their own stories, everyone pledging to go get tested, others condemning the catalyst as wicked, while some tried to play devil's advocate. It was a mess.

On the night that the post was "leaked", I came home to a quiet apartment. Khwezi's laptop was open on the bed so I knew she was in. Or that she had at least just been in. The screen was lit and active.

"Khwezi?" I called.

A slight rustle from the bathroom answered me, followed by a faint, "I'm coming."

I plonked onto the bed, throwing my shoes onto the floor. The laptop was open on the UCKAR student body page, on a comments section that ran down past the bottom of the screen. I had been working all day, with my phone on flight mode, so I hadn't received notifications from any social media thingies. But from this string of comments, I knew that something hectic had happened and scrolled up to read the original post.

The bathroom door opened and Khwezi stepped out. I didn't stop reading. It was unfathomable: people commenting about how someone, knowing that they were HIV-positive, had pulled off the condom while they were having sex, posters panicking, some posters I thought might have been crying while they typed. Whether because they had done something bad to someone else, had had something bad done to them, or were just afraid.

Khwezi was standing above me and I could feel her watching me read. Her breathing was ragged, loud and definite in the quiet apartment.

I glanced up at her: "Khwezi?"

Only my faint echo answered. I watched her close and open her eyes so slowly it felt like she was thinking about how to say something, anything.

"Khwezi?"

"Langa."

A person would have thought we were playing some kind of game.

I turned back to the laptop screen. "Khwezi, maan, sit down so we can look at this –"

"We should get tested."

A pause, my finger hovered over the PgDn button, Khwezi's breath hovered over me.

"Yeh?"

Although my head felt stiff on my neck and my heart was lurching as bile rose in my throat, I still didn't think I'd understood.

"We need to get tested, Langa."

We'd gotten tested already that year, at the start of the year like we'd done since we'd been together. But it had become more of a formality, a safety measure, none of us really believing that the results would have changed.

"I told you nothing happened between ..."

"It's not about that."

It was not like before. She was not questioning how far I'd gone with Mosesane. No. Now she was timid.

Yet, beneath that was a determination. A finality that we had to do this.

"Why then?"

"Why what?"

"Why do we need to get tested?" I wanted her to say it and wanted to know, although I wasn't sure why.

She shook her head softly, "Hayi, Langa."

"Why, Khwezi? Wenze ntoni?"

"It was more than two months that we weren't together. What did you expect, Langa?"

I didn't know what I'd been expecting. I did know that I felt struck. I told her this. I also told her I wanted to know everything: who it was, what happened, how many times.

"I'll tell you what I can remember," she said.

⁂

We drink. We get drunk. We have sex. These are ways of forgetting.

But I now have dreams of watching Khwezi walking slowly towards a woman, away from me, the sun dipping to rest as they kiss. This is a way of not forgetting.

⁂

At a high school. Behind it, rather. In a garden shed/a little room/umkhukhu. One of those portable buildings that weren't always part of the school, where extra books might have been stored. Or unopened rolls of toilet paper. Maybe even some brooms and mops.

There was a huge sign outside the school that read HIV Testing Centre (Open on Weekends). No hours. No specific days. Just open on weekends. When we'd arrived at the front gate, one of those green pointy boom gates, we found a security guard seated on a crate reading a newspaper.

As we approached the guard, Khwezi made a joke about the newspaper, a pun on the meaning of my name: "Maybe you're also a superstitious gossip, heh?"

It was difficult not to smile.

The guard, without looking up from her reading, knowing why we were there, instructed, "Go straight down the stairs. Turn left by the toilet. Straight straight straight until ibala. You'll see ngaphaya ekupheleni kwebala umkhukhu nyana nje, mara owamaplanga so."

We did. We clicked down the stairs following the strong acrid smell of what could only be a men's toilet. At its most pungent, we took a left, our shoes clicking down the quiet school corridors. Empty classroom windows surveyed us as we walked across the assembly quad. Straight, straight, straight, until the ringing of our shoes became muffled by grass. In the distance was a small white building. We moved towards it.

Right outside the door of the small room sat a woman in jeans and a white top. She peered at us over her glasses, reminding me of a lecturer who reminded me of my grandmother. She merely continued smudging her finger against her phone as we approached and also did not look up when we greeted her.

"Molo, sisi," Khwezi repeated, "We are here to get tested."

Almost as if she had not seen us coming, had not heard the first greeting, she peeled her eyelids up, lazily glancing at us, her eyes barely visible over the rim of her glasses. She rolled her head to and fro, her tongue plopping out to wet her lower lip before she spoke to Khwezi: "Okay, you can go in."

Her head lolled to the other side, pointing me to a chair I hadn't seen beside her.

"No, we are going in together," Khwezi clarified.

Now, her eyes twinkled, dangerously, excitedly, her swaying head and slithering tongue suddenly snake-like, poised and threatening. But she said nothing except "Oh!" followed by a drawn-out, disapproving clearing of her throat. "Ngenani ke".

The room inside was bare. Emptier than I'd anticipated. A row of metal shelves lined the wall right opposite the door. In front of the shelves stood a solid brown wooden desk, the kind you'd expect for a classroom teacher. Heavy metal filing cabinets in random spots; I had to dodge one as I sat down. It looked much like an abandoned office space, I thought. The kind that people went into to get documents from, like low-level insurance offices, with high windows that blocked out much of the sun. Only the short lace curtains did not abide by this aesthetic. Moving in the wind that blew in from the outside, they were delicate and ebullient. They looked like whispers.

At the desk sat a man in his late twenties. He was also wearing the blue and white which seemed to be standard, holding out his hand, palm up, as he introduced himself.

"Khwezi." A shake of the hand.

"Langa." Another shake.

He pointed to a couple of toy-like plastic trinkets on the table, "So, who wants to go first?"

A prick.

A rub.

Ten minutes waiting.

00:00:49

Do you guys mind if I play some music?

(*I shook my head. Khwezi was silently watching the curtains dance.*)

00:03:00

(*I picked at the skin around my fingernails. Khwezi still looking out. On the radio Michael Jackson was hollering about how bad he was.*)

"Are you nervous?"

(*I shook my head.*)

"You sure?" he insisted, "Most people are usually so nervous when they come here."

Yeah, sure. That makes sense.

Michael Jackson in my head.

00:05:00

"Anyways, you shouldn't be worried if you're not having sex."

"So are you guys friends?"

I shook my head. Khwezi was now gazing at me carefully.

"But you don't have boyfriends, neh?" (*Beat*) "Are you friends?"

No, I shook my head, We don't have boyfriends and we are not friends.

"Hmmmmmm, okay," his eyes twinkled.

00:09:55

"Okay, are you ready guys?"

He had covered the gadgets with his palms. Laughing, he waved them away, revealing the test results.

"You see! Both of you guys are good! Nothing to worry about."

In my excitement I forgot how upset I had been with Khwezi and beamed at her, the little light creeping into the room, whispering through the fine spaces in the lace behind her. He insisted on walking us to the gate.

Straight, straight, straight, all the way until the toilet instructed us to take a right and we saw the boom gate ahead and the guard's yellow and black uniform beyond the stairs. Before we parted, he strutted over and piped up: "I told you two. No sex, no HIV, heh. Now keep staying away from the boyfriends."

And, with a chuckle, he turned back down the stairs and we watched him disappear into the men's toilet.

⁂

Yes, I was happy. That neither of us was positive. Just because it was a good thing. Maybe, even more because I didn't want the ghosts of Khwezi's lovers to have a permanent place inside me.

⁘ ⁘ ⁘

Khwezi's lovers ... what an odd phrase.

⁘ ⁘ ⁘

There are enough ghosts that live with us already. My father's ghost does. So do her parents' spectres. At some point, I stop trying to get her to stand up to them, to her mother. The same way she stops hoping for a response when she asks about him, when she wants to know why I am sometimes so distant. Instead, I show her the care I have for her. I try to give her glimpses of all uMama is for me. In turn, Khwezi is there for me. She doesn't abandon me. We assure each other that we are enough for one another. We begin to right the wrongs of our parents.

⁘ ⁘ ⁘

#RUReferenceList

There were hushed whispers before everything exploded in Makhanda. I think there were signs even before the whispers came.

Makhanda always had this energy about, friction brimming with the ethereal. The air was always thick with anticipation. That week it was denser than usual, an atmosphere so heavy you could feel it weighing on your shoulders.

At least, the ache in my neck made it feel that way to me, and I rubbed my palm into my shoulder, trying to focus on the drone of my lecturer. The glaring red clock above him read 13:24. Nine minutes of me sitting there ...

I glanced at the empty seat next to mine. It was unlike Khwezi to miss classes. Late, sure, but not coming at all? My phone didn't have any messages from her either, so I typed in, "You okay?"

Before I could click Send, the unoiled shriek of the hall's door paused the lecturer's monotony midway and all the heads in the lecture hall swivelled to gawk at the latecomer. Khwezi entered the room. Anybody who didn't know her might have called her entrance a saunter, her backpack dangling casually off her shoulder, but I noticed a dizzy uncertainty in her eyes. Her smooth confidence attempted to hide the anxiety in her voice but was no match for me. I knew something was up when she said, "Sorry I'm late, sir."

Without a batted eyelid, he ambled back into his one-sided sermon and she to the empty chair.

"Look," she whispered urgently, shoving her phone into my lap as soon as she sat down.

Confused, I scanned the post on the Confessions Facebook page, "What is this?" I was trying to read without being obvious that I wasn't paying attention to the lecture. Khwezi was exposing my disinterest, pointedly watching me read.

"This is just a bunch of names, Khwezi. Who are th ... wait, isn't that ...?"

Khwezi's eyebrows were reaching right up into her skull, her emphatic nod screaming what her mouth could not.

"Koo-wear-zi, Lehnga."

For the first time, there was a glimmer of life in the lecturer's voice: "Perhaps it would be best if you two took this outside today?"

This time, everybody's eyes rested on us both. Before I could mutter my apologies and feign interest in his lecture, Khwezi was on her feet with her backpack in hand.

"Okay, sir, sorry about that. We will just excuse ourselves."

Her eyebrows prompted me to stand, too. When I didn't, she grabbed my sling bag and marched away, leading me past envious eyes and out the screeching door.

"Haibo, what is going on with you?" I asked, catching up to her brisk strides, "Can You Just Stop and Explain?"

She halted so quickly it took me a few seconds to realise she was standing behind me. I turned to her and she said, "Well, I mean, yes, those are people's names. Guy's names, it seems like. But think about it, Langa. Think about it ... why would someone just put up a bunch of names on the Confessions page?"

Most people were in lectures, but a few stragglers caught her tirade and appeared to be slowing their nosy steps. Like them, I didn't know what Khwezi was talking about.

"I wouldn't be asking if I knew, would I?"

She sighed, disappointed with my lack of crime-solving skills, "Okay, you don't know a lot of people on that list, granted. You do know Mavuso though."

I nodded yes.

"What has Mavuso been doing in your recurring dreams of him?"

I gasped, hurtled back into the grotesque cool on Mavuso's face in one of those dreams, "You think he – he –"

Khwezi pursed her lips, scrunching her eyebrows, and for the first time that day, her nod was solemn.

We walked home shrouded by our realisation, each wrapped up in thoughts and memories that felt entirely different, newly shaded. I was tugging at the memory of Mavuso grabbing at Khwezi, wondering if there had been more behind his bloodshot rage.

"Langa!"

Khwezi's calling sounded distant but present, repeated before I realised the memory had tugged harder than I had and dragged me into a stupor.

"Hmmm," I answered, rolling my eyes awake. There was a steamy film hanging over the street. I had to blink a couple of times before realising that it was rain.

Khwezi was giving me a concerned smile, "You just stopped walking. Are you alright?"

"Hmmmm," I repeated, pushing but failing to get my mouth to catch up with my eyes.

"Maybe we should go to the Rat and get a beer, just to chill out a little bit?"

I was grateful for the rhetorical question, and her guiding arm in mine as she led me to the bar. It was 2 p.m. on a Friday and the watering hole had a few customers having lunch and some casual day drinkers, like us. By the time our Black Labels arrived, I had my eye on the cricket game playing soundlessly on the flat screen above us. I gulped it down noisily, enjoying the distracting cool sliding down my throat before ordering another one.

"So, what do you think is gonna happen?"

She drew in her breath, lifting her shoulders.

"Do you think your dreams and I were right is the question?"

I bit my lip and she nodded again – it seemed her favourite gesture that day.

"We both know he did it. And even if we didn't know him, we know that these things happen and that people get away with it all the time."

The Proteas were getting pummelled and the camera panned to a very pink man, sunken into his seat, his South African flag hat also sulking. I couldn't help but smile.

"Point is, I don't know what's gonna happen." She added, "We will just have to wait and see."

✦✦✦

Another day.

"Langa? Langa, vuka!"

Khwezi's voice was in high-pitched panic mode, and my body rocked back and forth from her shaking my shoulder.

"Mmmm," I mumbled, trying to pull myself from my dreams. Trying but failing.

"Langa." She was annoyed now and no longer shaking me. Even with my eyes closed, I could imagine her sitting expectantly, head leaning against the pillow on the wall. Staring.

I grumbled. "It's creepy you staring at me like that!"

Without opening my eyes, I stretched my arm out to touch her, "What is–?"

My palms met the cold sheet. I forced my eyelids open, pushing my body to sit up. She wasn't next to me. Instead, our bathroom light was on and I could hear her shuffling around in there. Shouts and loud talking rang up through floorboards from downstairs, halted by another noise I wasn't quite sure of.

Louder this time, "Khwezi? What's going on?"

The bathroom door swung open and she strode into the room to stand with her hands on her hips at the foot of the bed. Eyebrows raised, she commanded, "Can you ever do what I ask, Langa?"

I furrowed my eyebrows, unsure what she was going on about. "I have been trying to wake you up for thirty minutes and even in your sleep you're still stubborn."

If she didn't sound so peeved, I would have giggled softly in response. Instead, I could make out her downturned lips in the light from the bathroom. She was dressed in dark clothes, jeans and a hoodie, and her dreadlocks were tucked into a beanie. A bright orange scarf was wrapped around her neck. A scarf. It was April, still so hot in Makhanda that we both slept naked with a flimsy sheet to cover us.

"Where are you going, Khwezi, and what is going on?"

Cutting me off, she said, "If you had woken up you would know what is going on."

I waited as she began searching around the room.

"There was shooting. I heard people shouting, screaming, and then these sharp, cracking sounds. It was shooting, Langa. And it went on for about ten minutes with people just yelling ... and ... and it sounded like crying, too."

I was still trying to wade completely out of my sleepiness. I looked at the duvet and cushions on the floor, our clothes thrown off in haste last night. I looked back at her, following her moving form as she opened drawer after drawer. I hoped I would find a way to respond to her before she found what she was searching for.

Finally, she pulled out her camera bag and checked to see if her lens was there. She saw that it was and came to sit on the edge of the bed, staring at me as I had thought she would when I woke up.

"Langa, they are shooting people now. I know, I understand that these protests haven't been easy on you. Even though you don't even want to talk to me about it. But –"

It was my turn to interrupt her, "I can't."

"We have to now, Langa. We have to stop being afraid and be there. It's not enough to know that we support the #RUReferenceList anymore. We need to actually be there now."

Her eyes were soft but insistent, eyebrows no longer bunched up. How much I wanted to just dive into those eyes and float away. I wanted to forget myself in their softness and forget all that I was feeling, everything that the past two weeks had dredged up.

As much as I wanted to, I knew I couldn't. Not even swimming inside her could wash away the blackness that consumed me. I shook my head.

"No, I am not going. You can do whatever you want. I know you won't listen to me anyway, but I am not going."

Khwezi bowed her head, biting her lip: "I will see you later then, okay?"

I wanted to ask her not to get up at all. Instead, I allowed my eyes to follow her again. She walked around the bed to the side I was sleeping on. I lay back onto my pillow and looked up at her. I wished I could beg her not to kiss me on my forehead, sweetly, as she knew it was one of my favourite things in the world. I didn't. I didn't say a word and she brushed her lips between my eyebrows. I wanted to go with her because I believed in the reasons she was going. I just couldn't. I just lay there, paralysed.

"See you later, Langa."

I just nodded softly and listened to her footsteps around the apartment, out the door, and down the creaky stairs as she left. And I just lay there, staring at the ceiling, hoping for sleep's relief. I just lay there and did nothing.

A few hours of gawking at the ceiling and TV, and some nervous messages later, I heard the telling creak on the staircase. The steps were slower than Khwezi's quick climb. I figured it must have been the older neighbour, but still rose to poke my head around the apartment door. The light from inside the apartment fell upon a dark figure moving up the staircase, face sheltered behind a hood. If not for the scarf over her nose and mouth, I wouldn't have recognised her. I edged out of the apartment into the unlit passage meeting her at the top of the staircase.

I mumbled a careful "Hi", waiting for her to reach me. Instead, she breezed past me into our apartment's warmth, leaving me in the murky outside, with arms outstretched. Inhaling deeply, I allowed the cool outside air to jerk me from my shock. I locked the door as the water broke from the shower, hiding the soft sobs behind the closed bathroom door. My feet moved me towards the bathroom, my mouth ready to beg her to open up, but that shut door said it all. It was giving me the biggest "sss" of my life and I could not overcome the shame that cooked inside me. Retreating, I opted for space, increasing the TV volume and noisily preparing breakfast.

Cinnamon oats and honey were set on the counter and the smell of eggs, toast, coffee and hibiscus tea was all about by the time Khwezi made her exit from the bathroom.

"Coffee?" I offered without looking up from the omelette I was busy with. It was doing that finicky thing omelettes do when they refuse to be pretty and perfect, forcing you to settle for scrambled egg and filling mess. I was not having it.

"No, I am not hungry."

My spatula hovered mid-flip, and I lifted my eyes to her. I could feel the tears poking out, shimmering onto my eyelashes. But there was no lump in my throat or shame, just prickly heat spreading across my limbs, brewing in my stomach, sprinting to my head, and jolting out of my mouth,

"What the fuck is wrong with you, Khwezi?"

She continued climbing into her pyjamas, wrapping her colourful doek around her damp head, before searching for her slippers. I knew she was intentionally riling me up, but I drilled on, circling the kitchen counter towards the bed.

"Do you think you are the only one who cares about what's going on because you can run around topless in the streets, huh? Does that make you better than the rest of us, Khwezi?"

She continued to ignore me, but her search was less pontifical now. She was listening.

"Not everyone can be you and your activist friends. We're not all brave and some of us don't want to be. I don't have to experience my anger in the same way you do. You think you know everything about rape, and rapists and anger and frustration when you don't. Well, I have news for you! Forcing people to do this the way you want is just as violent and invasive as forcing people to speak about what they have been through. And I will not! I will not and if that is not good enough for you then you should leave, but you will not make me ashamed about it."

I swallowed hard, panicked by my possessed tongue's outburst.

Khwezi looked as I felt. Her favourite funny word, *flabbergasted*, I thought. She looked flabbergasted.

"What did you say?" she asked, looking confused now.

"I said you are being insensitive and forcef–,"

"No, you just said something now. What did you say?" The hint of laughter in her voice.

I had said it aloud, "Flabbergasted?"

Her laughter asserted itself and invited me to join her.

"I" – (*laugh*) – "can't" – (*breath*) – "believeyousaid flabbergasted." Khwezi pointed through her laughter into the kitchen.

A thick plume seethed up from the stove, filling the small kitchen. Even as I ran to the stove, I knew my winning omelette had not survived. This time the tears bounded over my eyelids, staining my t-shirt, and landing on the ashy omelette.

Khwezi quelled her mirth and bounded into the kitchen, strung her arms around me and after a while peered down into my face.

"Who needs a shower when you can just cry into my chest?"

I smiled softly and pulled myself out of her arms. The smoke was travelling into the rest of the apartment – the ghost of dead omelettes.

"I am sorry for being insensitive and for wanting you to do things my way ... and for making you feel ashamed."

"I am sorry, too. For being bitchy about it. So will you tell me what happened?"

She pulled her lips tight into her mouth. "Maybe later. How about we enjoy this nice breakfast in bed instead? It is a Sunday after all."

Khwezi did not need to tell me what had happened. All social media was abuzz. It was week two of the shutdown by protesting students at UCKAR and they had used building rubble and tyres to barricade entrances onto the campus. Students took turns guarding the barricades and ensuring that the shutdown continued, but it was a Sunday and many students stayed in their residences, leaving smaller groups at each barrier. The police decided to take advantage of this.

In one of the videos, police attacked and physically assaulted a student, thrusting them against a police van even though the student was unarmed.

In another, two girls were shoved forcefully into a van and closed in. One of the students gasped for breath while another tried to help her. The police simply watched on.

I scrolled through different social media platforms, finding different scatterings of videos until I saw her dreadlocks dripping out from her hoodie. She was running away from the cameras and turned to look behind her before the screen filled with smoke and the pounding of gunshots.

Rewinding, I paused as a camera locked into her face, eyes wide with terror. I looked from the laptop screen to her sleeping face. Beside me, she was serene, most certainly of another world, shockingly beautiful. Yet, to some behind the 50 000 views, Khwezi was just another angry black woman.

✦✦✦

Charlie's favourite opening question greets me on Monday. This time he ponders my red, swollen eyes before posing it. "Do you want to talk about what's going on?"

This annoys me, often, about our relationship. Who he is, and who I am, and the fact that I come weekly to talk to him about my problems.

"Talk, Charlie? Don't you think there has been too much talking?"

I couldn't stop.

"Students are made to listen to speech after speech. The VC tells us about microcosms and government ministers and media outlets brand us hooligans. Our lecturers send us emails beginning with their declarations of empathy, ending in submission deadlines. The speeches we give to each other about changing things and holding men accountable are fucked. We talk and talk and talk, at hearings, for our reports, in your psychologists' rooms, like stupid fools in all these councils and commissions. Those that were arrested are forced to plead their cases to the very law they fight. The world lets us talk until we're all talked out, knowing that if we do anything more they can just shoot us down so that all we can do is lie in bed, drunk and drugged and numb.

"So isn't that enough talking for you, Charlie?"

For the first time, I don't back down from his intensely probing gaze and he breaks into the widest grin.

"No. No, I don't feel like you should stop talking."

He tilts his head and lifts an eyebrow, reminding me of the love that waits for me when I leave here.

"I feel like this may be the first time you've really spoken in your life, don't you?"

I roll my eyes and smirk. "Charlie, are you psychoanalysing me?"

For the second time in days, I burst into the deepest laughter, so warm it forms a bubble around me. And Charlie laughs with me as I weep and laugh.

⁂

There are others too.

You just can't run away from Cecil John Rhodes.

Not even impepho works for this fucker.

It's hard.

We come back home to him, sit in all our classes with him, witness his vices reincarnate in the powers that bring us to still-Grahamstown for our degree.

We are there when the protests erupt.

Not front and centre, but there.

So is he.

And when the protests die down he is stronger, a demon that terrorises us even in our sleep.

Rhodes and a system that molests and cons us into believing we are helpless, that we cannot overcome. But we also try to remember that in protest there is revelation, an exposure of truth, a coming out.

⁂

That not all protest looks like strength.

Every time we come home, every time we are together, we are coming out.

Even joy becomes resistance. Between the pain of being on campus. Between the tears we shed together, with our friends.

Amidst the bullets. In spite of the bullets. Even though Rhodes ... After all of the pain, we find a way to come home and be havens for one another.

In this way, we protest.

⁂

I envy everyone who can call home to sob.

There are not many of us here who can.

Instead, we are rocks on TV

with our arms raised, running, hiding.

Yet, still, no one sees we are only crying.

That there are no hooligans here.

There are tears in the bottles and stones we throw, the barricades erected, that what they call protest is a ceremony, a place for us to try and recover.

Our calls home are empty.

Sometimes more painful than the bullets, scarier than all the smoke, more alone than lying in bed listening to the crack of fire and the screams that will surely follow.

All we want is for our parents,

our aunts, our guardians to tell us it's okay, to help us breathe.

Instead, we must rely on lovers, friends and classmates who are also choking back panic attacks, dining, and falling asleep on triggers.

There is no time for us to be sad here, but every reason to be.

⁂

I want to call my mother. I am hurting. But there's no logic in hurting her too.

Rhodes is drowning me. In alcohol and pain. At least when I drink I can sleep. But even in my dreams I am drowning. I gag and gag and gag.

⁂

I sleep all day. The protests end. Lectures resume. I sleep. I know, "this degree is for the whole family". How could I forget? But the sun burns me, and the air in my lungs burns me. I am cremating all the dead things #RUReferenceList resurrected. If the people's Jesus could take a whole weekend to revive himself, I can be selfish. I too can take time to purge the sins of others.

⁂

Khwezi threatens to call my mother. I drink some water and call Charlie.

"What is going on, Langa?"

"I don't want to talk about it."

He is quiet before responding. "So why did you call me?"

"I don't know."

"You don't know?"

"I do know. But I don't want to talk about it."

⁂

Khwezi and I also lie hidden a lot, devouring each other. Sometimes I think it is too much, we should go and breathe the air outside. Until I remember that we are savouring. We are hoarding our existence together, so we don't forget when we go back.

Coming Out eKhaya

How does one "come out"?
What is the process?
Who is the most important person to know?
Why do we call it this?
To whom are you coming out?
And once you are out, who are you?
Are you different?
Are you new?
Are you not you?

10
eKhaya

As soon as the Greyhound bus leaves the small, bubbled-in disillusion of Makhanda, Khwezi and I begin the unconscious untangling from one another. We prepare for separate homes and different families. Her solemn eyes are reeling with all the memories she needs to recall, every reminder of "Do you still think you are gay?" that she must etch in the forefront of her mind. As the city nears, I witness her tearing herself apart, moving to believe in the prayers of her parents. They must not think she has changed, cannot detect any doubt when she reads their scriptures. She must not flinch when they shudder about a friend or fellow worshipper's child gone homosexual. Her eyes must not twinkle when she speaks of me. It is not safe. The further we travel, the greater the distance between us. By the time we arrive at Park Station, we are only friends.

✦✦✦

I had been back in Jo'burg a week and decided to pay Lungiswa and Nkosi a visit. Lungiswa was my cousin and the first person in my family that knew about Khwezi. Coming out is a difficult term to use for something you may not have actively hidden from someone. We lived in different cities and she never enquired after my love life. She and the world I had with Khwezi were separate. As most of my family were. Khwezi and I had been together for a few months when I told Lungiswa. I was visiting her in the apartment she shared with her boyfriend, Nkosi, in Melville.

Their warm reception was promising and hopeful. It coloured rainbows around the prospect of sharing myself with the rest of my family.

Lungiswa's voice pounded into the room, reverberating in my ears, driving me back into my seat.

"She's just confused."

My blood felt like it was vibrating across my body. Tensing up, I was contemplating whether to respond or to passively let them continue their analysis of my sexuality.

The three of us had spent the day binge-watching episodes of *Scandal*, and debating Olivia Pope's next move, pausing only to prepare meals and use the bathroom. It was a non-stop marathon. That is until Cyrus – one of the show's main characters – kissed H, initiating a steamy sex scene. I was caught in the intertwining of their bodies, their arms rushing to strip one another. Warmth slithered down my own body, trickling into my underwear. I was watching intently, slightly distracted, before realising that the scene was moving at an unnaturally fast tempo. Nkosi was leaning forward, fast-forwarding.

"I can't understand these people." His lanky body was folded into the small white couch. His skinny arms were rested across his chest and his heavy head hovered dangerously on his neck. It bobbed from side to side as he shook it to clarify: "These gay guys."

Lungiswa was quiet.

I retorted: "What don't you understand?"

I was worried his head would roll off, he was shaking it so vehemently. "It doesn't make sense how they can do that thing ... be like that."

My reaction was visceral, my body in revolt: my anus felt like it was being wrenched up into my stomach and the temperature rose beneath my eyelids. Nkosi had always seemed a nice guy, understanding, accepting. The words that launched from his mouth were words I'd never have envisioned from him. They were the words of angrier, more intolerant, people. And had they come from anybody else I may have allowed my tongue to pounce furiously on them. Yet, I forcefully placated it and guided it softly through my teeth before opening my mouth to speak.

Darkness silenced me. Load shedding.

Torch lights bounced off the walls as we searched for candles. Shadows lingered around me as I moved through the apartment. In the bluish rings of light, I continued to watch Cyrus unwrap H's suit. I imagined their dicks edging towards me in the darkness, their voices morphing into Nkosi's. Their shadows hovered over me chanting and moaning: "It's not right. It's not right. It's not right." His baritone boomed as their pleasured sighs rose. Intoxicated and jarred by the intensity, I stood in the passageway, my head filled with their merging chant.

Lungiswa fished me out of my mind: "Let's play Crazy Eight!"

The shadows and I floated back into the living room/kitchen area which was now amber in the candlelight. As my daydream slowly faded, we settled back into the couches. Nkosi shuffled the deck. I shifted in my seat. We played silently. Lungiswa lost the first round and rose to get some mango juice and snacks.

Nkosi shuffled.

"So why are you with Khwezi?"

The gurgling sound of juice pouring halted. I looked up at Lungiswa. She continued to pour the juice before chuckling: "What do you mean, baby?"

Nkosi turned to face her: "I mean, I know I love you and you feel the same right?"

Shadows bounced across the wall next to her as she nodded.

"That's normal," he continued, "I want to know why she is with Khwezi?"

I opened my mouth to answer. My cousin's voice locked in my own. She answered: "She loves her, obviously."

There was a khaki tinge to her voice: nauseous and uncertain.

Nkosi's head bobbed again. No.

"Girls only date other girls because they don't want to be with men because they've been hurt or something like that. Langa hasn't even been with a man."

"So I can't be with Khwezi because I love her?" I inserted before my cousin placed her own full stops into my mouth again.

Head bob. Bob. No.

My cousin's light brown eyes caught mine. I wondered if, beneath her careful placating of her boyfriend, she understood what my own eyes were saying to her. I questioned whether Nkosi's opinion reflected her own in any way.

Indirectly, she answered me: "Babes, Langa is not lesbian remember. She's – insert air-quotes – 'bisexual'."

"Actually, no," I began.

Lungiswa's chuckle interrupted me. She was sitting cosily in his arms, the candlelight dancing into the crevices between their bodies. She looked up at him and placed a gentle kiss on his lips: "She's just confused."

Only then did she look in my direction. Amber illuminated her eyes before they continued to debate when I would meet the right guy. I saw the reality of our relationship. She would always assert her answers over my own. Khwezi would continue to exist as a temporary stain, set to be removed when the light returned.

I left my protesting answers to wallow in the shadows. Lungiswa too, like Nkosi, refused to understand.

⁂

I was a loud, rowdy child. At family gatherings, bengivula ama-circle. I would call my mother's friends by their first names. I danced and ran around late into the night, until sweat dripped down my face. My family believed I would become iisbotho. I was the designated problem child.

This is the person my distant relatives anticipated when they met Adult Me emicimbini. "Do you remember me? I used to look after you when ..."

It's always interesting to watch the different reactions to the person I've become.

There is confusion, a misunderstanding. How could this be the same Langa who would have run in cheerfully greeting everyone with warm hugs?

Anger: "Lengane isiyazi qhenya nje. Does she think we're not good enough to talk to?"

There are also the disappointed, those who will shove stories and memories at me, trying to coax the extrovert Langa of their reveries out. Out of where?

My mother is embarrassed, sometimes. I see her close over awkward silences with her jokes, trying to steer people away from my presence. When she finds herself stuck, she speaks excessively, hoping whoever we are with does not try to talk to me.

I told her once when she asked me, "I don't know how to make small talk. If a person really has something to say then the conversation will happen. If not, silence is not a crime, Mama."

She looked at me as if she couldn't recognise me. As if, somehow, if she stared long and hard enough, she could begin to understand me.

My silence is not the only thing I think embarrasses my mother about me.

⁂

One and then two years passed. Khwezi and I were still together. uMama called me one day to tell me she had told my aunt Grace, her cousin. About Khwezi. Then uMama had told her other siblings, my aunts and uTa'mnci, who I'm sure had told their children. Soon, she couldn't even recall who she'd told. I didn't know who knew and who didn't.

A part of me was relieved. At least they knew, so coming out to them myself wouldn't be an active mission, a family-wide explanation I wasn't willing to give.

Yet, my mother's voice clawed at me. "Your uTa'mnci was so relaxed, I was surprised. It made me feel better. Can you believe he said I should be happy you're not doing Flakka or something worse?"

"Your aunt Grace – you know she's got that young girl that she's dating – she just laughed. I'm sure she was relieved that she wouldn't have to feel like the freak of the family."

Even though I knew she didn't mean to be ugly, that we wouldn't agree on everything, parts of me were disappointed in her, wounded. She wasn't as accepting as I thought she'd be.

A few weeks into my vacation and it was Christmas time and our family reunion was upon us. The same year she outed me, uMama was the sibling chosen to host it. We spent the week before scrubbing the house clean, polishing the windows, banishing any dust. For days, my hands smelled of bleach and Handy Andy. That is until Christmas Eve. That night I went to bed smelling of onions and Rajah.

On Christmas morning, Khwezi teased as she hugged me pressed against her car, "Unuka iKnorrox."

She pretended to peek into invisible pots: "Where's the meat? Huh? Heh? Where are the pots?"

"Mxm, kanti. Is that what you came here for? To tease me about smelling like the food I stayed up cooking for you?"

Coiling her lips, she pulled me closer, "I'm just playing, mudiwa."

Her blue Hyundai was parked outside the yard, ready for a speedy drive-off.

"Nervous?"

She shrugged, suavely arching her eyebrows.

Slipping my hand into hers, I tugged her gently into the yard, feeling her unwilling body edging along. The family was divided through the house. In the kitchen were the women, cooking and gossiping about other family members, some of them sipping ciders. Children under 13 played loudly in uXola's bedroom, teenagers and young adults in my room. The men were braaing in the back garden, chuckling louder and calling periodically, "We-Langa! We-Masindi! We-Lungiswa! Letha i-beer for uPeter. He just arrived."

"My grandmothers are in the dining room. We're going to see them first. The one in the red hat is uGogo Zonto. Greet her first. In the corner is uGog' Zantsi; compliment her, on anything. She loves it. I don't really know the other two but just smile and shake their hands, neh."

Khwezi looked baffled, like those swimming dogs on Youtube.

uMama was screaming, "Langa uphi?" Her shadow with hands on hips led her through the front door.

"LA-NGAAAAAAAAA! Where aaaare yyyy –"

Her eyes scurried from Khwezi, to me, to our hands still clasped together, and back to me.

"Molo, Khwezi." uMama did not look at her.

I squeezed Khwezi's hand. "Molo ma." Her nerves betrayed her now.

Pulling Khwezi closer to the doorway, I asked, "You were looking for me, Mama?"

We were a sandwich. I could feel my mother's hot breath on my face. It tickled my nostrils as I inhaled deeply. Khwezi's breasts were rubbing against my back. Up, down, up, down, up down with her breathing. The Christmas noise of my family felt distant: the chinking of pots on the stove, of celebratory toasts, the yellow laughter of the under-13s, igqom, "Hawu, kanjani Zonto", all the voices behind the doorway, and uMama, who refused to move.

"Mama."

Her breath smelled of garlic and onions.

"Mama, ndicela ugqitha."

Her chest rose. Up. And. Down. Up ... And ... Down.

"Mama." I ignored the glistening in her eyes. "Ndithe ndicela ugqitha."

✦✦✦

uMama stepped aside.

✦✦✦

Everybody already knew. I knew they did because they did not grin and ask, "Oooooh, what is your friend's name?" They nodded politely. They did not shake Khwezi's hand. She pulled it back the first two times. I told her not to offer it on the third. Only my aunt Grace yanked Khwezi in for a hug, asked her what her name was, sat her down to find out where she was from, what she studied and did for a living, all the things everyone else should have wanted to know.

She and Khwezi lounged in camping chairs outside, sharing a Hunter's six-pack between them as they spoke. I left them to talk, warmth cooing in my throat.

Until I overheard: "It seems like Langa is the boyfriend. That Khwezi girl is a woman, serious."

A reply: "Yuuuuuu, wethu amanyala wodwa. The things uLanga puts you through, sisi."

I stood outside the kitchen door, frozen to the wall. I recognised my mother's voice.

"Ye wethu. Whoever spoke of amanyala when your daughter brought her fifty-year-old sugar-daddy apha, hmm?"

Scattered giggles. Yewww. Cwaka.

Her scalding retort warmed my chest, spreading a grin on my face. Without thinking, I burst into the kitchen and, without acknowledging the other women, walked right over to uMama. The room was quiet, from the realisation that I'd heard their snide gossiping as well as the expectation of what I had come in to do.

I enveloped uMama into the biggest hug I could manage. The gravy-drenched wooden spoon she was wielding pressed into my t-shirt. When I finally pulled away, it made my front look as if my heart was oozing sticky red blood. I turned to face the confounded posse, and simpered, "If we wanted indoda, we would date indoda. But look how that has turned out for all of you. " Grabbing a biscuit from the centre of the table as I left.

I made my way back to Khwezi. She and my aunt were chuckling merrily; probably a soccer joke.

"Khwezi. Can we go please?"

Christmas. New Year. The festive season was fulfilled. My mum's defence was the warmest present. I didn't need to spend another minute there.

⁘ ⁘ ⁘

One of my uncles stayed on after Christmas. Well, not really my uncle. uTat'omncinci. A relative, kin.

I moved out of my room and into my sister's room, my sister into my mother's bed. To make space for uTa'mnci. He was to stay for a week, uMama said. The week she was working nights.

uMama had already left for work and Xola and I were watching Cartoon Network. *Adventure Time* was our favourite. I told her how I used to love *The Powerpuff Girls* which was coming on next, but that the newer version was not as great. The yellow talking dog on *Adventure Time* was getting married to a flying rainbow unicorn, singing his vows. We chuckled softly, humming along.

"Langa!!!"

I rolled my eyes dramatically at uXola. She smiled back. uTa'mnci was really beginning to irritate me. It was two days into the week he was staying and I had had it up to here. Every five minutes he was sending me somewhere, demanding something.

And because he was a guest and much older than me, I couldn't just ignore him. No matter how badly I wanted to.

"Eeeewee, Ta'mnci. Ndiyezaaaa!"

My room was the darkest in the house, in the corner of the yard crowded with large, towering trees. Light barely dodged past their shadows, even during the day.

"Why don't you turn on the light, Ta'mnci?"

I could make out his pudgy body in the dark. He was lying on his back, his large stomach jutting up towards the ceiling. Blue light from his laptop outlined him. I couldn't make out what he was watching.

"Light-a apho." He reduced the volume and placed the laptop down, screen facing away from me.

I clicked the light on, "You called me?"

He threw his legs over the bed's edge, patting the grey duvet cover next to him. My room looked different in the light, I thought. Rearranged. His bags were sitting in place of my shoes, his shoes lined up against the wall behind the door. I noticed he'd taken down some of my posters; my favourite one with Thandiswa Mazwai back in her Bongo Maffin days, with black lips and dreads. It was also quiet. No music playing.

Only tswiri-tswiri and the zzzzzz of mosquitoes. I could also hear the *Adventure Time* tune as the show ended.

He placed his arm around my shoulders as I sat next to him.

"Ewe, Langa ntomb'enhle. Bendikhe ndathetha nomama wakho namhlanje."

He kept clicking his tongue against his palate, a wet, slimy sound that stiffened my neck. I hoped he couldn't tell from my face how repulsed I was. *The Powerpuff Girls* tune began to play.

I knew he wanted me to ask what they had been speaking about but I couldn't trust myself not to tell him to stop with his tongue instead. I gave him the same smile I gave to white people who spoke English too loudly. Like when you have the flu and your nose is blocked.

"Well, she told me about your friend. The Khwezi."

His arm was now lower down my back, brushing up and down. It might have been comforting if I wasn't so taken aback by his statement.

"Ooooh ... Oh kaaay."

"Well. I wanted to know what was going on from you?"

I didn't know what to say and told him so.

"What is it about, Langa?"

His palm was now rubbing up and down my back. Up and down. I shifted forward, one bum cheek on the edge of the bed, facing him so he couldn't reach my back, trying not to make my discomfort evident.

"What do you mean?"

On my thigh now, scratchy. I wished I had worn pants. Or a longer dress. Xola's laughter twinkled from edining room. I almost tripped as I stood up.

With speed I'd never witnessed from him, he blocked the door. Grinning. Creepy teeth that reminded me of Sibusiso Dhlomo. I took a step towards the door. So did he, turning the key, pulling it out and placing it on the bedside table. Sitting back onto the bed, he picked up the laptop.

"Hlala phantsi. There's something I want to show you." I did not move.

Click, click, click as he increased the volume. He turned the laptop to face me.

"Is this what you do with her?"

My eyes bounced from the screen to the key. I could hear Xola laughing and talking to the TV. Moans came from the limbs and flesh on the laptop. He patted the space next to him on the bed.

I did not move.

The screen women howled with pleasure.

I did not scream.

They cried and cried and cried. Yes. Yes. Yes. Yes. Yes.

He rose, switched the room dark again.

I did nothing.

He just stood there grinning, dangling predator.

I did nothing.

He grinned and grinned and grinned. Xola laughed and laughed and laughed.

⁂

My heart is weeping. My head is weeping. My limbs. My ears. All of me. Why can't my eyes do the same?

⁂

"Yewethu! MO-LO LAAA-NGAAAA"

I jerked my eyes open to see uMama swapping her work shoes for slippers. A soft light shadowed the room and I realised it was morning.

"Why are you sleeping here?"

I rubbed my eyes, dazed, "Ma?"

"Why ulele apha and not in the bed?"

I glanced around the living room. The TV was still playing softly, and I noticed my bra on the floor next to the sofa where I'd slept.

"Ma?"

"Hehake. Utheni na?"

I shook my head, remembering, my vision blurring, hot. I ran my fingers over my face, feeling the spittle from the night before, the hot breath, "Ufuna ukwenza iSoddom neGomorrah? Huh?"

"Langa. Are you alright? Are you sick?" Her voice came through the liquid gush in my ears, a sharp buzz.

"We don't do things like this in this family," he grunted.

"Ta'mnci –"

"Langa!" they both called me.

"uTa'mnci, Mama ..."

"I will make this thing come out. It will come out of you. Ndizoyikhupha, out," his body insisted.

"Uphi uTa'mnci? Uphi?"

I heard and saw her slippers shuffle down to my room, the floodwaters rising up around me. When she returned to the living room, her brother trailing behind her, I rose to the surface and everything was clearer.

"Molo, Langa." He sat at the far end of the sofa, wearing the same clothes. His eyes twinkled a different greeting from the smile and voice. A dare.

"Molo, Ta'mnci."

uMama, oblivious, sat between us, "Please make me some tea, mntanam."

A spasm passed through my limbs as I rose, almost knocking me over. I cleared my throat.

"Me too, girl. Coffee."

Centuries pass in the present, and I feel them all, an itching apprehension yanking itself up my chest with every second I wait for the kettle to boil. Finally, I divide it into three cups, followed by fresh milk and sugar. The teaspoons tremble against the porcelain as I walk.

First, I stretch the tray out to Ta'mnci without looking at him. I can make out the musty, unwashed scent of him. The smell is nauseating amidst the intense coffee steam, causing the ball in my chest to rise into my throat. I move away from him and hand my mother her cup before settling gently onto the tiled floor. The cool of the tiles soothes me through my skirt, while the warm liquid softly guides my unease back into my stomach. As usual, uMama is sharing the details of her night shift. She volunteers every second week at a women's shelter which sometimes means helping out at night. This week she tells us of a young girl who came into the shelter, perhaps 18 years old.

The girl had run away from home for reasons she did not share and needed a place to rest for the night.

"She reminded me so much of you, Langa. Smart, kind, quiet, and ngathi unenqondo uyambona, it seemed." She sipped her tea contemplatively, “I wondered but didn’t want to push her about what made her leave her home.”

Ta’mnci shlurped his tea loudly, “Hayi, sisi. You never know with these kids. All I know is that they need a firm hand to guide them.”

His every word embittered my tea, leading each sip to invite that tightened chest feeling again. uMama’s “You’re right nyani, buti” punched it straight into my mouth. I sprung from the floor and the teacup splattered. I barely made it to the bathroom before my insides emptied into the toilet. I vomited until my throat felt dry, but even then I continued to retch, trying to get the last night out of me.

uMama stood at the door a while, watching me dry heave unsuccessfully. “Come, nontombi. Phakama. Ndizakwenzela itea emnyama. It will help relax your stomach.”

I obeyed, climbed into her bed and called Khwezi. She answered the phone with excited squealing. Yes, Yes, Yes! She wanted to tell some of her family about us, her sisters. I didn’t tell her what my family had done to me.

✦ ✦ ✦

It was a Tuesday, a teasingly cloudy day that allowed the sun to peek through briefly, only to trap it again behind grey rain curtains. We were meeting Khwezi’s sisters for lunch. They knew little about me, despite all I knew about them. At least according to Khwezi, who was driving. More importantly, they were about to become the first people in her family to know about us, about her.

Hues of dreams I’d had coloured my feelings. Yellow was most prominent. I knew exactly why. I was nervous, as I had been in the dream. “This feels like that dream.” Motes swimming.

She asked, feigning amnesia, “What dream?”

My answer: “The one I had about your mother. The one you haven’t wanted to talk about.”

White pushed against her skin, her knuckles protruding as she clenches her hands around the steering wheel. Sunlight refracted on the window a moment – the bright clarity reminded me of Khwezi's dream mother's coffee table. I tried to rub the images from my eyes. Colours fused behind my eyelids, the red of the couches, red in the frames and cushions. Lipstick on my lips: red. Yellow. The colour of motes dancing in the sunlight.

"What colour is that?"

Traffic lights switched red and we paused. Khwezi turned to look at me: "The colour of what?"

Concern in her voice.

"Are you okay?"

I shook my head forcefully, answering no to her question, but also trying to rid myself of this false, yet so convincingly vivid, memory. Trying to dilute the anxiety on her face I muttered, "How would you describe the colour of motes?"

"Motes?" We were moving again.

"The little dot-dots that you see in the sun sometimes. Like dust, but prettier."

She shook her head and asked me why. I told her I didn't know.

Palm trees introduced us to Sandton, long and luscious, pulling us up into the sky. Expensive heavens, I thought. Mirrored glass buildings shone and glittered in the light drizzle, as though sweating from the effort of being the capitalist and economic hub of the city. Suits darted across streets, communicated instructions on sleek cell phones, towed travel bags into the Gautrain station. Rain and great coffee sighed into the car.

One could believe that this was where gold and diamond carats were cut to cash.

Stepping into the petite corner café, I knew things wouldn't go as planned. We did not stand at the door and breathe, or hold hands to neutralise our nervous energy. There was no Colgate-gin kiss. Khwezi did not even look at me as we walked in.

Brown sofas, beige walls and light woods melted into one another and the café looked like a multicoloured chocolate sculpture. It smelled even better. Small groups of people were gathered over cakes and sandwiches reminding me of Gogo Zonto's gossip sittings. Laptops and gadgets angled open beside cappuccino cups at a few tables. Free wi-fi, I guessed. Kamva and Zenani were sheltered behind a sprawling pot plant, already drinking mango and strawberry fruit shakes.

"This is Langa. Langa, Kamva, Zenani," Khwezi introduced, gesturing to each sister. I held out my palm in greeting. They both rose to hug me.

I glanced at Khwezi over Zenani's shoulder: she knew I didn't enjoy hugs. Not from strangers, especially. We all greeted one another. There were smiles all round. Our waiter glided over to us. He reminded me of the palm trees outside, tall and soaring, with dreadlocks that spurted fountain-like from his head. Khwezi ordered a cappuccino. I knew I needed something stronger, some vodka, maybe even a painkiller, nothing I could find in a café menu. Two cappuccinos, please. I read his name tag: Clever.

They were all three studying in different cities. Zenani at UCT and Kamva at a boarding school in KZN. Listening as they caught up, I felt the dream coming back to me, the feeling of looking into Khwezi's coming out. Until then, I hadn't realised that Kamva was dressed in a yellow blouse.

"Would you like something to eat yet?" Clever's voice floated down. Three toasted sandwiches, a cheese omelette for me. He scribbled the orders, smiled, and moved to another table. Kamva picked up her handbag and glanced around at us: "Bathroom?" Zenani rose with her and I could feel bile rising to my throat as she did. Navy pleated skirt. As soon as they left, I turned to Khwezi.

"Khwezi, you remember my dream?"

Irritation rippled across her face.

"Right now, Langa?"

I nodded. "Your sisters are wearing the same things that your mother wore in that dream. The sunlight in the car. The motes. Us driving here nervously," I hesitated, "You coming out."

The first time I told her of the dream she had laughed and then been mad. I don't know what I expected from her. It definitely was not the quiet I was receiving now.

"Khwezi?"

"What do you want me to say?" She did not look at me and I knew she was surveying the bathroom door. She didn't want her sisters to find us talking about that dream. They would ask what we were discussing and she would have to share it with them. She would have to do what we had come here for, or at least I'd thought so.

"Why did you make me come here Khwezi?" I felt like all the mirrors on the buildings we'd driven past were inside me, like the sweating raindrops spilling, weeping down the glass windows.

Her hesitant non-answer gave me diamond-cut clarity: "What do you mean?"

The yellow and navy of her sisters' clothing blurred in my side vision. For the first time since we'd arrived, her eyes met mine.

"You're not going to do it, are you?"

Her eyes looked past me into those of her sisters. I watched her stutter back and forth between the three of us as they sat back down. Their confusion followed me as I walked out into the rain. Pick n Pay had a special on Jameson Irish Whiskey.

⁂

When will I realise that I must be a haven for myself?

⁂

She called me. I did not answer. I don't know if I can be her secret any longer.

⁂

I dreamt I was walking down a long street. It did not seem to end. In the distance, stood uTa'mnci noChris. At my side, my mother.

But as I continued to walk towards them, she faded away until they were at my side. I woke up; the bed was wet.

✦ ✦ ✦

Everyone makes a choice.

✦ ✦ ✦

uTa'mnci had left and everybody moved back into their corners. uMama came into my room and found me sleeping on the floor. I told her it was better down there. That I thought I needed a new bed.

✦ ✦ ✦

Days passing.

"Langa! Vula umnyango! Langa!"

✦ ✦ ✦

Weeks.

Ndiyacwila mama, I want to say. Please please come fish me out. Ndincede mama. My tears are drowning my heart. I might choke on the air I am breathing. Come and sleep with me, please. Maybe there will be light in my dreams with you here.

But I can't. I can't. I can't.

How do I begin to explain?

We are a family of thieves. uTa'mnci taking from me. Me, taking a bottle of Jameson from the Pick n Pay down the road. Maybe we are no different, he and I, maybe that's why I haven't told you, maybe I deserved it, maybe that's why Khwezi never thought I was enough to not be hidden, maybe I invite them, these men, these people that take and leave, they can't be coming for no reason.

Yes. Yes. Yes. Yes. Yes. Yes. Yes. Yes. Yes. Yes. Yes. Yes. Yes.

I deserve this.

✦ ✦ ✦

Am I being selfish? Yes. Maybe.

I was not selfish when I swallowed not being able to see her because she couldn't come, because her mother couldn't understand. I was not selfish when her father used to call and I had to be quiet in the home we shared because they didn't know we were living together. Be invisible. I was not selfish when I kept quiet about Ta'mnci in my bed. I thought of her. I did. All I wanted was to be seen by someone, someone important to her, anyone but her. All I wanted was for us to not be ruined by our families.

✦ ✦ ✦

I think so much I start to think that thinking might hurt me. I try to sleep but I think that even in my sleep I am thinking now. I see so much. So much that I didn't see before. Thuli, Khwezi's mother, hates the colour yellow because of the walls of her husband's mother's house. Because of Khwezi's father's mother's flowers in that kitchen. This is what I think about. Yellow reminds her of the day she hit her daughter. It is the colour of disappointment and anger. Maybe even the colour of pain for her. Maybe hate.

I think.

How can I ask Khwezi to battle so heavy a colour with her mother for me?

Is my not being a secret worth forcing that moment onto them both?

Can I continue to keep the colour from Thuli with Khwezi?

If I love her, if that is what this is, is this my burden too?

Yoh. Kunzima.

"Langa. uKhwezi is here to see you."

I opened the door. I realised how alike uMama and uTa'mnci are as she stood beside my lover. I told Khwezi she could leave, that I wanted her to. She did. She left me.

✦✦✦

"My mother hates yellow."

✦✦✦

I still remember how he smelled that day.

✦✦✦

Everyone chooses.

✦✦✦

On one of these days, I heard telling footsteps enter my room as I sat in the bathroom. I could tell by their landing it was my mother. I could also make out her shuffle as she glanced about the room, looking for clues. I caught the sounds of her rifling through the soiled sheets on the floor next to my bed.

She lifted one urine-soaked bunch of sheeting. "Kwenzeke ntoni, Langa?"

The tea she had brought with her was a sandwich staring at me through the steam. I refused to answer, so she turned her attention to her feeding mission. We sat down to our tea. I focused on the ripples in my cup as I blew into it, avoiding her eyes on me, ashamed, uncertain what to say to her.

"Is this about uKhwezi?"

She did not stumble or hesitate before saying her name. Nor was she cold and distant. It sounded like she really wanted to know and, glancing at her, I noted an interest, a saddened curiosity. Not the relief to see my relationship with Khwezi fail I thought I'd find there.

"Langa, mntanam. Relationships are not easy ..."

I could not believe it: empathy plus advice, hhhe banna.

"But you must decide for yourself which challenges and whose baggage is worth fighting for because there is no human that does not have problems. And I might not understand you and uKhwezi but ke," she smiled tentatively, "that girl is not an alien, and she cares about you."

Chuckling, and through hot eyes, "An alien, ma? Really?"

"Heeyyyi, ndikunika i-advice etops wena all you hear is *alien*? Ngumntana otheni na lona bethuna?"

"I thought you didn't like uKhwezi."

"My opinion about who you love is exactly that. My opinion. But it will never stop me from supporting you."

I weighed my troubles with each nibble of my sandwich. She was right, somewhat. All people had relationship issues, though different. This I could tell her to ease my thoughts and expand the space for the thing that she would find impossible to bear.

When I finished sharing the story of meeting Khwezi's sisters, uMama cleared her throat and declared, "Well, I already knew. I just wanted you to tell me when you were ready."

"You knew what?" I retorted.

"Well, Khwezi told me what happened the day you chased her away from here. And she left you a note."

"Which you read, I'm guessing ..."

With childlike embarrassment, she explained, "I was worried about you."

I nodded my understanding, "Where is the letter?"

✦ ✦ ✦

Langa,

It has come to me how scared I have been of your dreams, how much fear has made me flee from knowing ... Do not think I did not see what happened the last day I saw you. It has not been an easy thing, has it, this thing between you and I? It has been full of love and passion and care. Hope even? But easy, no. And there have been many reasons for this.

My fear, one of the biggest.

I thought I was ready to move past it. I believed I was. I was until I saw your dream in front of me. How could I look at them, my sisters, without seeing my mother in that yellow? How would I tell them who I am and who you are to me without being afraid of what they would see? And how much like her they looked in those clothes.

I cannot be sorry that I am fearful. I have had every reason to be this way. But I am sorry I could not make you feel like less of a hidden thing.

Thank you for being an open home and for all your patience.

Uyathandwa ndim.

Khwezi

⁂

It had been a week and a half – maybe two, I did not know – since I'd last spoken to Khwezi, more since uTa'mnci. uMama had scraped together a grocery list, to get me out of the house, I knew. At the small mini-mall near my house, I spotted Mosesane's red car. It could have been a look-alike, but I'd memorised his number plate, remembered it from our drives.

Leaning against the back window, he was embracing a short, plump woman, smiling down at her jokingly, the same warm, uninhibited lips he used to share with me.

That is why I'd let him kiss me that day. I knew that as I glared at him and her across the parking lot. "We just kissed," I had said to Khwezi. But it was more than that. He had uncorked feelings and moments Khwezi had reserved for the beginning of our relationship, brief clips of freedom and recklessness; kissing at sunset, traffic in the background, dancing in the drive instead of inside with our classmates. With him, I was always "out". There was no hiding. That is why, when he kissed me, at the gate of his home the day I told him I was with Khwezi, his neighbours staring as they passed, knowing his mother was in the yard, I did not falter, nor did I stop him. I kissed him back because I could, because his lips did not fear mine and I wanted to. Because we were free to.

Yet when you had that freedom, I thought as I waved at him, you passed it over because it was not enough.

⁂

Revelling in the success of getting me outdoors, uMama forced me to accompany her to Gogo Zonto's. I was in the kitchen making tea even though they probably wouldn't enjoy it, uMama and uGogo in the living room. I caught snippets of their conversation, knew uGogo was telling uMama about someone who had died, a funeral that was coming up. Sliding the teacups and pot onto the tray – uGogo wanted the whole shebang – I intruded into their chat.

"She killed him. Bathi she took a knife from the kitchen wamugwaza. And then," uGogo made a scissor-snipping gesture, "she Cut. It. Off."

She added as she smacked her hands together, "Konke."

My mum gasped at all the right points, devouring the gossip she always enjoyed with her mum. I couldn't help but join them. I wanted to know who lost their penis.

They were surprised when I asked, "Who is this, Gogo?"

All was still when she answered. Everything. The breath in my lungs. My heart. The blood in my smallest vein. I was certain I must have been dead or dying because all I could see was Black. Absolute darkness, nothing else. Leaving the tea, and grabbing my bag, I left the house. It was Saturday. Mavis' tavern was booming, I knew. I needed a drink.

⁂

It was grimy there. The place I was in when I woke up. I could make out people in some of the beds along the walls. It was a long dormitory, the sun weakly slipping through the curtains I was sure had once been white. I was in an asylum, I thought. I knew. The same place they had sent my other aunt after her son got run over and died. My mum had given up on me and sent me here.

I heard talking outside before she came in. Arguing, yelling at someone it sounded.

"Stupid visiting hours," uMama greeted. Her nose twitched when she lied or was hiding something. It twitched when she said, "Alcohol poisoning."

A hospital. Not an asylum. She was still hiding something though.

"Mama, what's going on?"

She scratched at her nose.

"The doctor said I shouldn't say anything that might upset you." I'd never heard her voice so soft. So careful. "That you didn't remember because ... because sometimes your brain chooses to forget certain things. He said we shouldn't say anything to you about what happened."

I hardly cry. Because of her, because I never see her crying. Now, I felt as though I was witnessing an anomaly, like snow falling.

"Mama?" Keeping her with me in the present.

She shakes her head, brushes the tears aside. Not now, she is saying. "No."

I am firm. It shocks her, pushes her into the chair next to my bed. It jolts me too.

"No, Mama. Talk."

I find out he was a known rapist, uChris, that the blackness he blanketed over my life was something he would weave and spread on a regular basis. The girl who killed him was one of his victims, others were coming out to tell of how he had done the same or similar to them too. The police were saying this girl might have to go to jail for a while, unless we all testified. Then she might receive a lighter sentence. The girl who killed uChris, castrated the rapist, exterminated the pest, purged the sin, might be sent to jail. I pondered: what a way to thank our heroes.

"The girl did not lie about Chris. She did not lie."

I set my eyes on her but she would not look back at me. She is scared to know, I see, scared to ask how I know but I tell her anyway.

"I know because he did something to me, Mama. I don't remember what he did but I know he did something a long time ago now. And I will have to tell the truth to everyone so that they can believe that girl."

I know she is crying although she tries to hide it behind her bowed head. Swiftly digs a tissue out of her bag, dabs her eyes and looks at me. Her nod says *I have heard you and I will support you*, and the hug that enfolds me when she leaves confesses *I am here for you if you need me*.

uMama signs a few papers and because I am doing well, I am allowed a day pass for the funeral.

uMama arrives at dawn, with a black dress and jacket over her arm. She also brings me some fruit, and I nibble as she zips me into the dress.

The ward is eerily quiet, the click of our shoes the only sounds as we exit into the yard. It's a grey day, Xola would say, clouds low and grumpy, the air smelling like angry rain. Our drive is just as quiet, radio turned off because uMama can't stand it when she's feeling pressured.

She'd been asking me all week why I would want to attend the funeral. Each time she brought it up, I could see she had been crying about it and it made me question my decision to go.

"I just have to Mama." I gave her the same answer as before.

It was a long drive and the longer we drove, the more I realised how much I missed being outside. I'd been holed in for so long, drowning in myself, that I'd forgotten how magnificent being outside could be.

My phone vibrated in my lap and I unlocked it to read the text:

> Hi Langa. It's been a while since we've spoken and our last meet was up in the air with the protest action on campus. Are you still in Makhanda? How would you feel about a session if you're up to it? It can be virtual too. Let me know. Thinking of you, Charlie.

As usual, Charlie's timing was clairvoyant, a swooping Superman when I needed one. But I wasn't ready to talk. I pressed the power-off button, blacking out his words in annoyance.

Irritation must have poisoned my expression because my mother asked, "What's wrong?"

I shook my head to indicate nothing, but my tongue opposed me: "Why do men always have to want to involve themselves?"

She half-smiled, "What man is this?"

"Charlie." I read her confusion and added, "My therapist."

She nodded, "But isn't that his job?"

It certainly was. Knowing I had no answer other than it annoyed me that I liked, and shared my fears and troubles with, a white man, I pursed my lips and shrugged.

"You know ... I went to therapy once."

I did not dare turn to look at her in case my gaze stopped her from continuing. So I focused my eyes on a scratch in the passenger window glass, using my silent attention to prod her further into talking.

"Yes, I did before your father – you know ..."

"Left. He left, Mama."

"Yes. Ndaphantse ndaphambana yilandoda nezimanga zayo."

She was about to cascade into one of her "your-father-was-a-dog" tirades, so now I cast her a "that's-not-the-point" look. She inhaled firmly and continued.

"Yes. Being with him was not good. Not for him and not for me because I did understand him and he didn't try to understand what I needed from him. It was just what you kids call toxic."

Now, I couldn't help but smile at her, so genuine in her efforts to understand at times. Failing, often. But also trying, often enough.

"What was your therapist's name?"

The car swerved for a moment before she righted it, overcome by a remembering laughter. I watched the changes in her face with each breath that fed her mirth, and recognised again my first-ever love.

When her breath finally settled her back into herself, she smiled, reminiscing.

"Your father used to bring that up when we were disagreeing just to make me melt a bit ... How could I go tell our business to a woman with such an ugly name? And I would cry from laughing. Her name was Priscilla."

✦✦✦

Chris' family home is a small four-roomed brick house. Not many people arrive for the burial and the family does not seem to expect more because they begin the service early.

"That's his mother," uMama's whisper points to a woman poised in the front row. I keep my eyes trained on her as the short list of speakers present their eulogies. Not a single tear leaks from her face. Not even at the graveside, as umfundisi speaks.

"We hurt our children," he says, "We don't listen to them when they try to speak to us. We forget why God gifts them to us. And when it gets too much, we turn our backs, question how they can do things like this, how they can take life, how they can be so cruel. When sometimes it is our fault. May his soul rest in peace."

I don't know why I chose to come here. I know I didn't have to. I know that people will stare and point, that his family will feel more pain with my being there. Yet, I watch as they lower the casket into the ground, into the blackness. I feel unburdened and proud.

His mother is invited to scatter soil into the grave. After she does, she turns to look steadily at me, with a precision that implies she knew exactly where to find me. She turns away from her son and comes to stand before my mother and I, speaking first to uMama before turning to me and saying, "I am so sorry."

Without waiting for a response, she leaves. Shortly after, so do we. We climb into the car and I immediately switch on the radio. I lower my window and stick my head out as the car speeds into the road. Like a wolf, I howl crazily and shrilly, turning my face to the sun. I am warm, light and revitalised.

Adrenaline, I think. Who cares?

I howl heartily and uMama joins me until we chorus into a high laugh. We stop back at the hospital and she admits, "I've always wanted to do that."

I wink at her before jumping out, "Me too."

✦ ✦ ✦

The wild abandon was short-lived. I lay thinking in my cot that night, if I had done, or said, something before was it possible there wouldn't have been others? Maybe. But where do you begin with broken memories and incomplete, incomplete nightmares?

✦ ✦ ✦

I dream again of the long street that does not seem to end. In the distance, stands uTa'mnci. I carry a shovel in my hand and, at my side, my mother wails and howls and moans like a dog. She watches as I dig a hole so deep into the tarmac that the rest of the road disappears. Her brother crawls down into the bottom of the hole and lies there. His eyes threaten to strangle me but he does not move. Instead, he begins to weep and wail as loudly as his sister who is then muted by his voice. We stand over him and as he wails below, my mother begins to call my name. He bawls – she calls me and shrieks, screams out my name.

"Langa!"

I quiver awake to see uMama's twin face look down at mine, my mother earnestly pulling me back to reality.

Sobs gurgle from my throat and I cry. I cry and I cry and I cry. uMama holds me. She is my light. I do not tell her about uTa'mnci. I am not yet ready to be the one to have to comfort her.

⁘ ⁘ ⁘

She had been standing in that doorway for a while, I knew. It was her way of being. Gogo Zonto would blow into a room softly, and catch you like a lingering cold. When I was younger, she would sit and watch me being naughty, stealing biscuits, eating powdered milk from the tin. She would loom unseen and then just as she thought I was done, she would announce herself.

Langa.

Gogo ...

Pulling her handbag tighter to her side, she wafted in, glancing about at the other beds in the long room. She moved through the room, greeting as she passed each bed, stopping and staring at me when she finally arrived. "Sawubona, Langa."

"Sawubona, Gogo."

Neither of us liked small talk, my grandmother and I. We sat, staring at each other, her perched on the rickety metal chair beside my bed. Her phone chimed and she dipped into her handbag, pulling out a blue plastic "Nay' ibanana". She continued digging, eventually pulling out her tilili.

A pause as she read the text. She sighed, annoyed, "Mxm. These loan people, always trying to take our money."

I could tell she was tempted to start playing games on the phone; her favourite pastime. We didn't really have much to talk about, I thought.

"Umama wakho ungitshele ukuthi uloku ungalali?"

"Yebo, Gogo."

"Kwenzenjani?"

I shrugged, something she would have chastised me for usually; Awunamlomo yini?

"Uphupha ngani?"

I told her. About my dreams. I knew she knew, that burying her nephew was not a good omen here. We sat in silence, staring at one another. I wondered if she was going to do anything. Part of me hoped she wouldn't. But I also wished she would.

She didn't.

We sat in silence until the nurse came in to announce the end of visiting hours. She left me as she had arrived, with the instruction to eat all twelve bananas and finish them.

+ + +

So it's a surprise when, the following day, I lift my head to see her leaning against the doorway watching me. She is wearing a pastel mint-green two-piece with a creamy yellow trim, a black hat and brown brogues. Her handbag is sandwiched under her right arm, a bursting plastic bag weighing down her left.

"You've been in that bed too long. Get dressed, we are going for a walk."

I dare not question her. The halls are livelier today, patients enjoying their lunch in different corners, the isolated visiting friends and family. I push open the front doors, holding them open for her to parade through, and parade is the only way to describe the sassy confidence of her walk.

It is a sparkling sunny day, sunshine glinting silver on the plants in the facility's gardens. I follow her to a concrete bench and table set beneath a large tree and sit at the bench's edge, half in shadow. There are people seated on the lawns and all around us on garden benches. From her plastic bag, Gogo brings out a banana-apple-mango-grapes fruit pack, a lunchbox with two sandwiches, Tropika, her floral tea flask, and two plastic cups.

From habit, I hold out cupped palms as I did when I was a child. She gives me one of the sandwiches and pours herself some tea and, for me, Tropika. We eat quietly, watching birds flying and insects skittering about. When she has finished, she dusts crumbs from her skirt and turns, angling herself to face me.

"I spoke to your mother last night and told her my suspicions about your dreams of your uncle."

She pauses, thinking aloud rather than expecting an answer. Eating my sandwich suddenly feels more interesting and I focus my eyes on little brown specks in the bread.

"I know what my son has done, and –"

I have never seen Gogo Zonto cry, and knew I wouldn't today either. What I see in her eyes is the closest I might come. But her eyes do not waver when I meet them.

Clearing her throat, she declares, "And I will not protect him. I will not apologise for him and I will not defend him, but you must tell me and your mother so that we can defend you."

She reaches out and places her palm on my back, rubbing it gently. It feels like she is massaging renewal into my chest, each rub sweeping away all the dust in there. Cobwebs fade beneath her touch and from my clean thoughts, I recollect a question I have long been afraid to give life to in speech.

"Gogo, why did uTata leave? I saw him the day that he left and he never even said goodbye. Why did he leave?"

We are the last in the garden, others strolling unwillingly back into the building as visiting hours near their end. Her rubbing falters at my question, then steadily continues again.

"Your father was a very unwell man, in many ways. He had his flaws and liked women before, which caused a lot of disagreements with your mother. But even after he stopped with abafazi, they still fought a lot."

I help her clear up as she speaks and we head back towards the front door.

"He had too many urges and one of them was to always be wandering, looking for something or somewhere. He would vanish for days and weeks. At first, your mother would get hysterical, fearing for his safety. But the more it happened, she would simply get mad. The week before he left, she had told me that he said he wanted you all to move to Durban. He had no job there, no house, nothing, but he insisted you up and leave. Even though your mother said no, the need continued to claw at him and he left."

We pause at the double doors.

"Your father, I think, kept so many things inside him that anytime he was still keeping them inside too long, they swallowed him up. Akufanekanga ugcine izinto phakathi ezibuhlungu. That is what made him leave. And that is what has made you sick now. Do you understand?"

"Yebo, Gogo."

I stood at the door and watched her parade down the stone driveway, out the gate and down the street. She turned when she reached the corner and waved before she disappeared.

⟡ ⟡ ⟡

Therapy, long-distance.

"Hi Langa." His waving palm filled the screen and I waved back gingerly. "I am glad you texted me back."

Honestly, I had had no intention of doing so. It had been weeks of upended turmoil and pure, well, shit, and Charlie had a way of picking at my anxieties and nudging me to look right at them. We sat for a while in silence, only three minutes the video call claimed, and when I said nothing, he prompted, "How's home?"

It was a slimy feeling, that clamouring ocean that answered his question. It flooded my limbs, rushing into my chest, bashing my lungs in. The roar that it induced sounded nothing like me. It took hold of my body in waves and shudders that culminated in that raw, deafening sound. Once it had faded into a satisfied mumble in my throat, I told him everything. Not in the allusory telepathy of my grandmother. Nor with the tears I wept with my mother. I spoke until my eyes were as dry as my throat, and the painful hum of my chest was no longer. Without waiting for anything more, since I finally felt like we had reached the point in our relationship that I had been chasing since I started seeing him, I closed our call with a "Thank you, Charlie".

Understanding me as he had always done, his reply sealed our ending. "Don't sweat it."

✦ ✦ ✦

FAMILY MEETING.
I stood behind uMama, who stared into her lap. uGogo spoke.

MINUTES OF THE MEETING.
My grandmother's living room was full of flowers. The curtains were a dull peach, lacy, a floral pattern. Porcelain vases with bright porcelain bouquets decorated a wooden shelf. A white tablecloth with faded pink roses was spread over the wooden dining table. In the centre of the table were the only real flowers in the room, in a glass vase.

Six pairs of eyes turned towards us as uMama and I entered. She sat next to uGogo, opposite uTa'mnci.

ATTENDEES.

uTa'mnci. uMama. uGogo.

And some other adults I only ever saw at funerals and weddings and Christmas.

uMama encouraged me to stay in my room.

"No, Ma."

So I was there too.

MEMBERS NOT IN ATTENDANCE: Xola.

Business.

Motion from one of the other adults to hear what happened both from me and from him.

A counter from uGogo who claims she knows what happened. She continues to describe to the attendees, the details of my dream.

Another "other adult" scoffs and argues that we cannot speak of people's dreams as reality. Let alone the dreams of a young girl like me.

uGogo counters, states that I have already spoken to her and any statement from me is unnecessary. She puts forth a motion to hear from uTa'mnci. There is no counter motion.

uTa'mnci was wearing the same green, yellow and white jacket he always wore. The same one he was wearing last time. And the same look that bordered between a smirk and a wounded dog's grimace. His hands dangled beside his chair, hidden from my view over the edge of the table. I could make out blue jeans as he shifted slightly. Maybe the same but probably not. I let my eyes trickle over all of him, slowly soaking him in: his neatly trimmed haircut, the faded acne scars on his cheeks and forehead, the small scar on his chin, an abnormally large nose, I realised. His lips were chapped and slightly grey, and occasionally his tongue poked out to wet them. His eyes, I could not make out. He did not look at me, not once. Not in my direction. Not at uMama. The only person he looked at was uGogo. At some point, I saw tears leak from those ugly eyes that now chose not to see me.

* * *

On the day before I was discharged, another visitor. Unlike Gogo Zonto, I heard her before seeing her, her enthusiastic greeting of the staff and eruptions of her audacious laughter. By the time she entered my room, I'd tied up my hair, moistened my lips with balm, and sat up in my bed, pretend-reading. One of the women in a neighbouring bed giggled softly when I feigned surprise.

"Khwezi?"

She passed "Good afternoons" and "Molwenis" around the room before coming to sit beside my bed, laying a bouquet of tulips across my lap. She beamed at me and her eyes squished into slits, pushing tears onto her cheeks.

"Hello, Langa."

I couldn't help but return her smile.

"I've missed you."

I shut the book and set it on my lap. "Yes, I've missed you too ... And I got your letter."

I knew she had so much more to say. She always did, and I wondered what she had been up to since I last saw her.

Instead of swamping me with all her stories, she asked me how I had been and when I did not respond said, "I am sorry, Langa. I am. And I want you to trust in me again, I do. And I realise now how much I have not considered you too, and have led you on and been an asshole. Well, the last part mostly being the words of my sisters and –"

"Your sisters?"

Khwezi nodded, "Yes ... I told them about you. They can't wait to see you again. And to meet you properly." She added, nervously, "That's if you still want to, of course."

I wanted to act cool and nonchalant but my face must have betrayed my ecstatic shock because a chuffed grin broadened her face. It quickly vanished when I quipped, "That's good for you, then, that you told your sisters."

The flowers she'd bought were sunshine in each petal, a deep golden yellow, streaked with fiery orange and crimson. I lifted them up to my nose and could have sworn they smelled like citrus. The memory they invited lingered on my lips and I looked up at the woman I shared it with, knowing that was why she chose that bouquet in that hue. In the look we exchanged was time and love and a friendship filled with the blessings that coloured all my dreams.

I forgave her. She forgave me too.

✦✦✦

I woke up at sunrise on my discharge day, the sun tip-toeing around the room, tentatively brushing against the edges of people and objects. It poured in from the window at the head of my cot, shining over my head through the thin curtains. I looked through its rays at the ceiling, shimmering motes and mellow yellow making me feel like I could float right up and dissolve into the sunlight, into a world beyond the ceiling.

What would it feel like to go home now, after everything? Would Ta'mnci still wait for me in my room?

I swung my feet off the cot, pushing the thoughts away and my feet into my slippers. Everyone in my ward was still asleep. I tried to creep softly to the door but the slippers betrayed me with an occasional thwack. A few grumbles and moans complained about the sound even though nobody really woke up. The corridor was just as peaceful and asleep, the nurse on watch overcome and dozing in her chair.

My slippers threatened to tell on me. I pulled them off and slid in my socks out of the front door. The sun outside was braver than inside the building, embracing rather than brushing over the world. Flowers and plants in the garden smiled, the old building glowed youthfully in its rays, and the sand, the grass and the windows shimmered with dew. All about me even the air felt transformed by that light. I ran into the garden, my socks drenched in the wet dew, droplets of it spilling down my arms from the tips of spiky leaves. I stood in the garden and looked up at the sky's blue, so ravishing and endless.

The sun firmly touched my arms, one hand and then another, and kissed both my cheeks and my forehead before wrapping her many arms around me. She held me, spreading warmth and life back into my body. I let her welcome me back into myself. She let the tears fall from my face and dried them when she knew I had cried enough.

Langa, she asked me, are you well?

I closed my eyes, No, no, I am not. But I will be.

Yes. But you will be, she agreed.

⁂

Purple jacaranda blossoms rained down onto the streets, blowing in through the open window, forming clusters of petals all over the car. A slight drizzle was also falling onto the windscreen, stray droplets spraying onto my face. Through the trees, the sun beamed yellow. A monkey's wedding.

The car smelled of damp mud and spring. As we turned onto Luis Avenue, Khwezi poked her arm out the window, water sticking petals onto it, the sun making light bubbles of the droplets. Her house was right at the end of the street, enclosed by tall, thick trees that pushed out the sunlight and multiplied the rain with their quivering leaves.

I pulled into the driveway which was not as prim as usual. The wind and rain had shaken leaves onto the ground, weaving a green rug. Branches and pieces of litter dotted the green and specks of brown mud dotted the grey walls. I let the car rumble on.

"You okay?"

Khwezi nodded, pulling her arm back into the car. She scraped off the petals, letting them fall onto the car floor.

"We can still leave?"

"No."

The engine sighed off.

Her house looked exactly as it had the first time I'd been there. The startling white. How clean it was. A mix of lavender and bleach rising from every surface. Except that Khwezi's parents were in the living room, her mother reading a magazine, her father watching TV. I was surprised by how cosy they looked with one another. My imagination had conjured up an image of them as cold, distant people who did not enjoy physical touch and only relaxed when they lay in bed after their nighttime prayer.

Yet, here they were; her hair weaves hanging lazily off his knee, his hand gently rubbing her stomach, both thoroughly engrossed in their inactivity. Her face was buried into a magazine's pages. His face lit up as soon as he spotted us, with a smile so akin to Khwezi's it made me gasp slightly.

"Hallo girls," he chimed.

She rose smoothly from his lap, leaning back into the sofa, allowing him to leap up and extend his palm:

"Anesu, ndiani shamwari yako?"

I almost exclaimed, who is Anesu?

Khwezi reminded me of her second name as she responded, "Baba, this is Langa. Langa this is my dad."

We shook hands and he insisted I call him Uncle Lot.

Chuckling, he added, "It is a nickname for me because people say I never look back once I have decided."

We all three turned to look at Khwezi's mother who only glanced at us briefly over the edge of the magazine when her husband introduced me. Khwezi and I settled into the two armchairs opposite the sofa they had been nestled on. Laughter tickled my throat when I saw the madams from the Real Housewives gossiping on the TV. I eyed Khwezi and she gave me a faint smile.

"So, Anesu," her father began, "You said you wanted to speak about something?"

I watched her nod and push her front teeth carefully into her lower lip. She tugged at a dreadlock between her fingers.

"What is it, Khwezi?" It was the first thing her mum had said, and she surprised me again. Her voice was so soft, almost mellifluous.

Khwezi glanced at me fleetingly, before looking back at her parents, and then at the TV. I reached for her hand, calming it from its fidgeting. Her palm closed around mine and she turned to look at me. A million corny phrases invaded my head. Probably, a billion in hers. I nodded and offered a smile, instead.

She bobbed her head back.

Thuli had placed the magazine on the glass table, and she and her husband gazed at us, although each with a different eye. In him, I noted confusion and bewilderment. If he were a colour, he would have been a purple darker than jacarandas, tinged with a frustration that echoed when he asked again, "What is it, Anesu?"

Thuli's shade glinted in her eye, the dawning of memories bright and vivid in her stare. She did not speak, did not flinch, did not move a single muscle in her face, it seemed. Only her eyes darted from Khwezi to me, back to Khwezi. I watched them, mother and daughter, watch one another, really look, really see. And I knew they were back in that kitchen, birds cawing in the sunset, stew bubbling on the stove. As Thuli rose, all she could see was yellow, I knew.

Yet, still, I hoped that she would laugh dreamily, nod, too and ask, "Tea?"

Coming Out To Myself

There are books on everything you need to know about weddings: dresses, hairstyles, décor, themes. Books are written to teach people how to date, how to play players, how to think like men. People write about all sorts of things: dogs, plants, colours. The world is abundant with knowledge and guidance where it is needed. Yet, in the search for enlightenment about coming to yourself, the oceans of wisdom run dry.

The people I'd have thought to ever speak to about my experiences showed themselves incapable of understanding. Perhaps even unwilling to. Books, which I'd always turned to, spoke very little to the situations that now presented themselves. There were some, but certainly not enough.

To Khwezi, I said: When you become a writer, please write a book about us. Our stories are worthy.

✦✦✦

My mother hurts me. I don't tell her this. Maybe it's because I'm scared our relationship won't survive all the things I have to say to her. About Khwezi. About more. I think I'm more afraid she will leave me.

✦✦✦

She will never leave me. She loves me. [Un]conditionally. And she is trying. I know this.

✦✦✦

I have a good family. Sometimes. But when they are bad, it jolts me. I feel like I am coming apart.

✦✦✦

I was always wary Khwezi wouldn't choose me. She didn't. But in many other ways, she did.

✦ ✦ ✦

The world scares me. So do so many truths. I am a coward. I am also brave.

✦ ✦ ✦

I don't like the colour black. Maybe I never have. It reminds me of my uTa'mnci who dirtied us. It also reminds me of the trauma I buried.

✦ ✦ ✦

I hate the colour blue. It reminds me of my father who loved the ocean more than me and left.

✦ ✦ ✦

Forgive your parents. You will find bits of them in everybody, in all your lovers, in yourself. You cannot live resenting them. It only means hating yourself.

✦ ✦ ✦

We can have a love that thrives even beyond our dreams. We can love and must. For all the hate we cannot escape.

✦ ✦ ✦

Sometimes I felt so broken being with Khwezi. Not because of her. Because of everyone else.

✦ ✦ ✦

In this lifetime, nothing I do will ever be "normal". Not as long as I can love a vagina and the heart to whom it belongs, as I have loved Khwezi's. That is a burden and a daily fight I am learning to accept.

⁂

Colours are the dreams you recover in everything you look at.

⁂

Khwezi, remember, ulilanga.

⁂

Langa, khumbula, you are light.

Acknowledgements

This book burst out of me unexpectedly and speedily and once that fast shock of it was over, it stayed to grow as I grew. Through it, with it, because of and for this book, I discovered the people that live within me. It is them whom I must thank above all, for giving me the words, the dreams and the faith to make this happen. Nangikhanyisela indlela.

Next, I must thank my mother, Noncekelelo Jeyi, for her love and for giving me the space to break all the limits I thought possible. My father, Mxolisi Ximba, for staying with me, his support and his presence in my life always.

My friends, Lesego Ntsime, Luncedo Ximba, Sindiswa Ximba, and Lungisa Madywabe, for holding space for the good and not so great parts of me. I love you, guys.

Thank you to Mary Armour and Colleen Higgs for seeing the potential in this work and for their patience. Lalu Mokuku and Dr Siphokazi Magadla – for nurturing this book without knowing it.

Finally, thank you Yali; Tau Ya Mariri. Because of you I have learned how to love myself and how to love others. Through and with you I have discovered how boundless this world is and how amazing it is yet to become. Thank you for believing in me. A thousand times over.

Praise for *Dreaming in Colour*

An elegantly expressed coming-of-age/coming-of-queer treat that tackles the questions: How does one explain gayness to their immediate community, if at all? More importantly, how does one explain to their own guilt-ridden subconscious that these feelings of love and desire are just as legitimate as any other, that it is ok to live in one's truth? *Dreaming in Colour* does not answer these questions for us but rather exposes the reader, through its protagonist, to the bedraggled yet colourful magic of queer life. A pertinent and necessary contribution to current literature.

—**Chwayita Ngamlana**, author of *If I Stay Right Here*

This story is a cornucopia of queer experiences that looks at navigating the confusion that is intimacy, sex and identity. A thoughtful take on a timeless story of love, belonging and a search for self.

—**Tiffany Kagure Mugo**, author of *Quirky Quick Guide to Having Great Sex* and curator of *Touch: Sex, Sexuality and Sensuality*

Printed in the United States
by Baker & Taylor Publisher Services